Dear Reader,

Welcome back to Blackfoot Falls! In the second book of this series we revisit the cozy Montana town, the Sundance Dude Ranch, the McAllister family and sexy sheriff Noah Calder, who's so popular with the female visitors, he's ready to lock *himself* in jail just to get away from them. But once he finds mysterious Alana Richardson, Noah won't let her out of his sight.

You'll also meet Dax, Noah's lovable mutt, who is based on one of my rescues. Dax is a Border Collie mix who is full of love and mischief. And just like me and my Dax, Noah can't imagine a life without his four-legged buddy.

Many of the Blaze authors and editors have come together to support pet adoptions via the Blaze Author's blog. Come visit blazeauthors.com/blog/blaze-authors-pet-project to see the many incredible ways we humans can band together to help our furry friends.

I'd also like to invite you to spend your Christmas holiday with the McAllisters and all the folks from Blackfoot Falls by picking up *On a Snowy Christmas Night,* which will be out this December!

I hope you're having as much fun with the gorgeous cowboys of Montana as I am!

Love to you all,

Debbi Rawlins

Debbi Rawlins

OWN THE NIGHT

HARLEQUIN®
entertain, enrich, inspire™

Recycling programs
for this product may
not exist in your area.

ISBN-13: 978-0-373-79717-2

OWN THE NIGHT

www.Harlequin.com

Printed in U.S.A.

ABOUT THE AUTHOR

Debbi Rawlins lives in central Utah, out in the country, surrounded by woods and deer and wild turkeys. It's quite a change for a city girl who didn't even know where the state of Utah was until a few years ago. Of course, unfamiliarity has never stopped her. Between her junior and senior years of college, she spontaneously left her home in Hawaii and bummed around Europe for five weeks by herself. And much to her parents' delight, returned home with only a quarter in her wallet.

Books by Debbi Rawlins

Prologue

RACHEL MCALLISTER STARED at the Sundance Ranch website she'd created, feeling more helpless and overwhelmed than she cared to admit. Three months ago she'd taken the first reservation, her fingers crossed, prayers murmured in earnest that opening a dude ranch would help pull her family out of the hole. Now they were so swamped with business she didn't know which end was up. It would've all been good except they didn't have the room.

Sure, the ranch spread out over three thousand acres, but they raised cattle first and foremost, and she'd promised her brothers she'd keep the guests separate and under control. So much for that. The women had gone nuts over Cole, Jesse and Trace, and the other young cowboys who worked and lived at the Sundance.

Now, after the first few waves of visitors had sampled life under the clear blue Montana skies, they were writing fantastic reviews. Cole's new girlfriend, a former guest, was a popular travel blogger and she'd talked up the Sundance on her site.

All of it was terrific for business but brutal on Rachel's stress level. Already she'd oversold one weekend and pissed off two women. They had nobly offered to take up residence in the bunkhouse with the hands for the two overlapping days, but that would've pissed off everyone else on the ranch.

Rachel clicked on the latest batch of reviews, skimmed down and smiled when she repeatedly saw Noah Calder's name. The sheriff was Cole and Jesse's best friend and like another brother to her. He wasn't going to be happy about his fifteen minutes of fame—especially if women started swarming his office.

Well, that would be his problem. Rachel had enough on her plate. She hoped she wouldn't regret accepting guests until three weeks before Christmas. Initially they were going to close from the first of November until the first of May. But it was just too damn hard to turn away the business.

Naturally, she'd have to come up with other activities to offer the guests. Summer was easy, with hiking and camping trips, white-water rafting, cattle drives, fishing, rodeos. Early fall could include some of those things, at least before the first snow, but up here in Blackfoot Falls, Montana, almost two hundred miles from the Canadian border, the temperatures dropped early.

Her computer dinged with the receipt of an email, and she was surprised to find a last-minute cancellation. Well, that worked out great. She had just been about to turn someone down for a week's stay starting tomorrow night. Quickly, she did the paperwork, and feeling magnanimous, returned the deposit, then booked the new guest. And that was it for the night. She was exhausted.

Before she turned off her computer, two more reviews caught her eye. More Noah fan club members.

Review by: Tammy from Chicago
**** 4 out of 5 stars
I spent a week at the Sundance in August. Sheer heaven. Never thought I'd like going to the Wild West

but could've easily stayed a month. My friend dragged
me. I totally owe her flowers. Beautiful scenery. The
food was way too good. Best of all, the cowboys were
smokin' hot, and not just the brothers on the website,
who were even better-looking in person. Lots of cute
wranglers, and if you go, get a load of the sheriff, a man
who knows how to fill out a uniform. I'm saving up to
go back next year. I would've given the place five stars
if someone had hooked me up with that hunk wearing
the badge.

Review by: Miranda from San Francisco
***** 5 out of 5 stars
OMG I just had the best vacation ever! I like horseback
riding and hiking and I'm basically an outdoors kind
of gal. All the activities the Sundance offers are super
fun, and the best part—Trace, the McAllister brother
with the tan Stetson in the home page photo, was totally
hands-on and yes, he's as gorgeous as he looks in the
pic. But don't overlook Sheriff Noah Calder. Make a
point of visiting Blackfoot Falls, about half an hour
away. There's a quaint bar there called The Watering
Hole. And did I mention the sheriff? ☺

Rachel grinned. Trace ate up the attention, but poor Noah.
He was going to head for the hills.

1

ALANA RICHARDSON HAD PRECISELY one hour to vacate her office. She kicked off her new Christian Louboutins, swung her stockinged feet onto her desk and stared out the large glass windows at her perfect view of Madison Avenue and Saint Patrick's Cathedral. The autumn sky was more gray than blue, but the trees compensated for the drabness with their orange and yellow brilliance. Normally October was her favorite month. But not this year, not with the move from Midtown to Tribeca, with which she was in total disagreement.

She was the newly appointed vice president of marketing for an ad agency that had laughed in the face of recession. Partly thanks to her, they'd increased their net worth by fifty percent and had outgrown the twenty-first-floor office that was more home to Alana than her Upper West Side apartment. Though sentiment had nothing to do with her attitude toward the move. What she objected to was being sidelined for an entire week. The whole transfer of files and furniture and computers could've happened in two days if her boss had been more reasonable.

She flexed her toes. Damn, her feet hurt. The four-inch heels weren't the problem; for her those were standard. They put her at six feet and brought her eye-to-eye with, and sometimes taller than, most of her male coworkers. She liked the psychological advantage. For some of her peers it didn't seem to matter that she was at the top of her game, or that she worked harder than anyone else. They thought she was too young, too green to have moved up the ladder so quickly.

At least no one assumed she'd slept her way into her position. She wasn't unattractive, but she was no great beauty, either. She simply didn't have the kind of face and body that made men stupid enough to pass out unearned promotions.

Her office door opened, no knock first, which meant it was her assistant, Pam. Alana turned from the window and eyed the blonde's jeans. She hadn't wasted any time in shifting out of work mode. "I thought you were coming to tell me you were staying in the city with me."

Pam tilted her head to the side. "Let's see…skiing in the Alps with Rudy or working fourteen-hour days with you. I'll have to think about that for a second." With her usual deadpan expression, she checked her watch. "You can still come with us. Our flight doesn't leave for another four hours."

"Pass."

"So you're going to stay cooped up in your apartment and work."

"I've been meaning to see *Wicked,* and that other one…." Alana waved her hand. "That musical with what's his name."

Pam shook her head in resigned dismay. Young, only twenty-five, she'd been three years behind Alana at Yale. But she was sharp, ambitious and didn't miss a trick. That's why she'd been hired twenty minutes into her interview. She reminded Alana of herself. With the exception that Pam had the good sense to spend a week in the Alps and regenerate, while Alana planned on burying herself in ad copy.

"I want to show you something, and I need you to promise to keep an open mind." Pam moved around the desk, shoving Alana's feet off and taking over her keyboard.

"I'm not promising anything." Alana rolled her chair back to give her assistant room. Though Pam seemed distracted by something under the desk.

She dragged out Alana's wastebasket and sighed at the remains of the desktop Zen garden Pam had given her as a stress reliever. The sand had fallen to the bottom of the basket and the miniature wooden rake had snapped in two. "I see this worked well."

"Actually, it did." Alana smiled. "Trashing the whole thing felt remarkably soothing."

With an eye roll, Pam went to work, her fingers flying over the keyboard. She brought up a website and stood back. "Check this out."

Alana scooted closer, squinting at the startling expanse of blue sky above a huge log-cabin-style house. In the lower corner of the screen were three cowboys, but it was one of their horses that caught her attention. With that lean, powerful body and a shimmering gray mane, he looked like an Arabian, but she couldn't be sure from the picture. What was this, anyway? Her gaze went to the top of the screen. The Sundance Dude Ranch.

It took a second for the words to register. She narrowed her gaze on her assistant. "A dude ranch. Me. You're kidding."

"Why not? You like to ride. Do it where the air is clean and men are men."

Alana laughed. "I haven't been riding in years." She slid another look at the three cowboys. Not bad, if a woman liked the rugged outdoor sort....

"All the more reason to get your overworked type A ass out of the city and do something fun for a change."

Groaning, Alana swiveled to find her shoes. "Remind me why I keep you around."

"Because I don't take your crap, I'm very good at what I do, and I know how to fix your computer," she said, then point-edly added, "without erasing the entire hard drive."

"God, I'm going to hear about that for the rest of my life."

"Take a damn vacation, Richardson. You need it."

"A dude ranch. Sure thing." She winced, trying to stuff her foot back into the narrow shoe. It had to be the correct size. Her personal shopper had chosen them, but they were new. Alana had figured half a day's wear would be enough to break them in.

"Look, I probably wouldn't have thought of it on my own, but I have friends who went last month, and they came back raving about the place. Plus they said the guys were totally hot."

"You have time for friends? Obviously I don't work you hard enough."

"Just read some of the reviews."

"Yeah, I'll do that."

Pam exhaled in that long-suffering way she had perfected. "You are so myopic."

Alana quit trying to put on the shoe and brought it up for closer inspection. Her eyes were tired from another late night reviewing ads, and the print was too blurry. "This is an eight, right?" She showed the toeless black pump to Pam.

"That's not what I meant." Clearly annoyed, her assistant ducked her head to glance at the size. "Yes," she said, her expression changing to one of banked amusement. "By the way, your mother called while you were meeting with Mr. Giles."

That was odd. Eleanor rarely called the office. Alana opened the desk drawer where she kept her cell and saw that she had several messages waiting. "And?"

"She's lecturing at a conference in Boston this weekend. After that she's going to the Cape for a few days. She wanted to let you know she'd be away."

A sick feeling churned in Alana's stomach. "You didn't tell

her about the move," she said, not liking the knowing gleam in her assistant's eye. "Or that the office would be closed."

"I'm not sure." Pam frowned, but couldn't quite keep a straight face. "I might have mentioned it. Was that wrong?"

"I'm not afraid of her." Not a *total* lie. *Terrified* was a better description. The woman wasn't a monster, nothing like that. But if Alana thought *she* was good at manipulating people, Dr. Eleanor Richardson was the damn master. Nine out of ten times she could get her only daughter to crumble like a stale brownie. And if her mother knew she was free, she'd insist Alana accompany her to the Cape. "I can say no to Eleanor."

"Of course you can." Pam grinned as she moved around the desk toward the door. "But you know, with all the fall foliage, Cape Cod is gorgeous this time of year...."

Sighing, Alana dug out her phone. All three messages were from Eleanor. Oh, crap.

"Have fun with Mom," Pam said on her way out with a wave over her shoulder.

"That was so beneath you," Alana muttered, loudly enough for Pam to hear, then drummed her short, pale, manicured nails on her desk while staring at the phone as if it were the enemy.

She had to call her mother back. If she didn't, Eleanor would inevitably show up at Alana's apartment. The doormen all knew her. They'd probably lay out the damn red carpet without even giving Alana a heads-up that her mother was in the building.

And why not? Eleanor Richardson was beautiful and charming, a world-renowned psychiatrist who knew exactly how to get what she wanted. With her expertise perpetually in demand, she was wined and dined, courted by some of the most prestigious institutions in the world. The woman knew no humility, though Alana marveled at how well her mother hid her arrogance and sense of entitlement. Her ability was truly something. Almost enviable.

The thought made Alana shudder. She loved her mother and respected her because she really was brilliant and worked hard—her discipline was an amazing thing. But Alana didn't want to be like her. Eleanor had no friends. Never in a hundred years could Alana imagine her having a conversation like the one she herself had just had with Pam. It was a small thing, perhaps, and there were many qualities passed on to her from her mother for which Alana was grateful.

She also appreciated the top-notch education she'd been provided, the fabulous trips abroad, the trust fund that guaranteed she'd never have to worry about her future. But the perks had come at a price. A normal childhood had been the trade-off. No sleepovers or going off to summer camp or attending Friday-night school football games like her classmates. No father to read her stories or tuck her in at night.

When she was younger, Alana had thought often about how her life might've been different if she'd had a more traditional upbringing. She'd even considered inquiring about the man who'd fathered her. One particular time she'd been so furious with Eleanor for planning a Caribbean trip for them the weekend of the junior prom that she'd nearly asked her mother why she'd bothered having a child.

But Alana hadn't asked. Instead, she'd sneaked out of her room late that night. She'd made it only five blocks in their posh neighborhood when the police picked her up, assuming she was whacked out on drugs, given the way she was furiously muttering to herself. When they'd returned her home, Eleanor hadn't raised her voice, not even an eyebrow. She'd merely opened the door, thanked the police in that cool, elegant voice of hers, while Alana raced up the stairs to her room.

Until dawn she'd waited in agony for her bedroom door to

open, for Eleanor to lash out at her. The lecture never came. She hadn't been grounded, no privileges were taken away, and later, when they'd sat across the table from each other while the housekeeper served them breakfast, Eleanor had smiled that charming smile she'd perfected, and reviewed the itinerary of their Caribbean trip as if nothing had happened.

It was then that Alana recognized the truth of their relationship. She'd finally understood her role. Eleanor hadn't necessarily wanted a child; she'd needed a companion. Marriage had never even been considered. After all, what man could meet her expectations?

But a child? Perfect, really, because it gave Eleanor the opportunity to mold Alana into someone who suited her mother's preferences. Infuriatingly, the plan had worked far too well. For all Alana's good intentions, she ended up bending to Eleanor's will far too often.

Alana blinked at the monitor when the unimaginative galaxy screen saver obliterated the picture of the Sundance Dude Ranch that had been there a second ago. She touched the mouse and recalled the website, her gaze sweeping from the beautiful Arabian to the cowboy straddling the animal. Hot guys. Right. What was Pam thinking? She knew Alana's taste was more sophisticated than that, in clothes, in men....

Although she had to admit these were some pretty nice specimens. She moved in for a closer look at their faces, but two of the cowboys had their hats pulled low. The third one had his brim tipped back and was very good-looking, but on the young side. They were the McAllister brothers, owners and operators along with their sister and mother, according to the blurb. The ranch had been in the family for several generations, but only recently had they opened their doors to paying guests.

Alana had to smile. Yeah, she'd just bet the place was popular, especially with women looking for a vacation fling.

Out of curiosity, she clicked on the descriptions of the activities offered and, impressed, started skimming the reviews.

Just as she figured, the ranch was solidly endorsed, and so were the men. Some of the guests had included photos of their vacation, and Montana was undeniably beautiful country, with breathtaking views of the snowcapped Rocky Mountains, open meadows and storybook streams. Though the highlight for most of the reviewers had been—big surprise—the men who worked the ranch. A whole slew of photographs were dedicated to the brothers, the hired hands, the town's sheriff....

She peered closer. Yes, she could understand why some women might find Sheriff Calder appealing. Alana wasn't one for a man in uniform, certainly not half a uniform. Along with his official tan shirt, he wore scuffed cowboy boots and worn jeans—wore them quite well, in fact. But it was his strong, chiseled jaw that caught her fancy, even if his sun-streaked brown hair was a bit too long.

Her phone buzzed, signaling an incoming text.

She pulled open her drawer to check the display, though she knew who it was, and that she wasn't about to answer.

Eleanor's message was brief. She'd be in a meeting for an hour, but needed to talk to her immediately after.

Alana's gaze moved back to her computer screen and the blue Montana sky. Outside her door she heard laughter. The mailroom staff had been assigned packing duty, and it sounded as if her office might be next on their list.

Montana, huh? God, was she seriously considering this? Was the idea too crazy? She pushed her fingers through her hair, trying to recall when, exactly, she'd last been horseback riding. But a dude ranch?

Hell, why not? She wasn't allergic to fresh air. And she was getting tired of sailing in the Caribbean and visiting the Hamptons. Not that she ever had much leisure time.

Who was she kidding? She felt like a teenager again, trying to ditch her mother. The thing was, she hadn't really lied to Pam. Technically, Alana could say no to Eleanor, except the woman had a way of digging in her claws and making Alana feel guilty as hell. Sometimes it was just a look, a single word, a lift of a brow, and Alana was toast. She'd try not to give in. She'd call herself every kind of fool, because in all other aspects of her life she had a spine of steel.

But when it came to her mom, the end result rarely varied. She'd beat herself up for being weak, throw in the reminder that Eleanor was a psychiatrist, for God's sake, even without the power accorded all mothers to elevate or scar their children well into adulthood, if not for life. Alana would feel better for a few minutes, but then eventually give in and do what Eleanor wanted.

Might as well wager on a dude ranch halfway across the country, on the off chance she'd actually have fun. Except no one could know, absolutely no one. Image was everything in Alana's business. Hell, her client base consisted primarily of sophisticated trendsetters and Fortune 500 companies. No, she thought as she clicked on Reservations, not a single person could know. She wouldn't even tell Pam.

NOAH CALDER STEPPED OUT OF HIS office and peered down Main Street. The Lemon sisters had finished decorating the *Gazette's* window for Halloween, and moved on to hanging paper ghosts from the elm tree in the stamp-size park in the center of town.

Normally, he would have gone home by now and left the evening shift to Roy. But it was Friday and the boys from the Circle K and the Double R had been paid earlier. Half of them would end up at the Watering Hole to shoot pool, get drunk, and mostly hang around hoping to get lucky with one of the women staying at the Sundance, who often ducked into the bar.

In general the men behaved themselves, but Noah had promised Rachel McAllister that he'd keep an eye on her guests. Though to his way of thinking, it was the men who needed looking after. Most of the gals who'd been coming to town since the dude ranch opened weren't the shy type. They knew what they wanted and weren't afraid to ask for it.

A couple of them had scared the hell out of him. Offering to buy him drinks, asking to take him to dinner or to go on moonlit rides… One bold young lady had asked if he'd take her somewhere to go skinny-dipping. And now even his deputies were giving him grief over it.

He turned to look the other way and muttered an oath when he saw Avery Phelps bearing down on him.

"You listen to me, Sheriff, and you listen good." Flushed from spending too much time sidled up to Sadie's bar, Avery shuffled down, shaking a scrawny fist in the air. "All this thievery business is on account of those McAllisters. And I ain't the only one who wants to know what you're gonna do about it."

Sighing, Noah shoved Avery's fist out of his face. He was in no way threatening. In his prime, Avery might have topped off at five-seven, but age had him bent and bow-legged and a foot shorter than Noah. Even so, he knew the old man was harmless. Annoying as hell, generally belligerent, and probably lonely since his wife of fifty years had passed on three winters ago, but he wouldn't hurt anyone.

Noah met the old-timer's bloodshot, beady eyes. "I suggest you think about how you're phrasing that accusation, Avery."

His brown weathered face creased in confusion and he swayed to the left. With a light touch to his shoulder, Noah brought him back to center. The guy was still active, but damn, he felt frail.

Hell, Noah didn't need something else to worry about. Since he'd moved back to Blackfoot Falls, his plate was full enough with his aging parents. They were the main reason he'd returned—that and he didn't care for city living. "Why don't I drive you home?"

"I got my own truck. How else you think I got here, boy?" Still frowning, Avery rubbed his whiskered jaw. "Don't go mixing up my words, either. I ain't accusing the McAllisters of thieving, but it is their fault things have gone missing, what with them inviting all them strangers to town."

For three months Avery and his cronies had been ranting about the influx of tourists, and Noah was getting damn tired of it. Although part of his irritation had to do with the fact that he hadn't made any headway in solving a rash of thefts that had plagued the county since the McAllisters had opened their doors to guests.

Sure, the economy was bad and a lot of folks were out of work, but he knew most everyone for miles, and they were good, honest, God-fearing people. Transients had come through looking for work over the summer, but the timing was off. They'd all been long gone before the first theft occurred, so he knew they weren't responsible.

Some of the stolen property had been recovered, but no thanks to him or his deputies. Harlan Roker's trailer had been abandoned in a field ten miles south of his ranch. The Silvas' water truck had gone missing for two days, then turned up in back of Abe's Variety Store.

It almost seemed as if someone was toying with Noah, showing him they could do whatever they wanted and he couldn't stop them. But he'd been sheriff of Salina County for three years, and to his knowledge he hadn't made any enemies. Yeah, he'd broken up the occasional bar fight or been called to settle a squabble between neighbors, but nothing serious. He'd worked as a Chicago cop after the army and college, before returning to Blackfoot Falls. Normally he could handle the job here with his eyes closed.

"Look at 'em." Avery pointed a gnarled finger at a green rental car that pulled up in front of the *Salina Gazette*'s office next to the Watering Hole. Three young blondes dressed to kill climbed out.

"Quit pointing."

Avery ignored him. "That's when the trouble all started. When that *dude* ranch opened. Those damn McAllister kids... their poor father is turning over in his grave."

Noah forced the man's arm down. "Shut up, Avery, or I swear to God I'll lock you up on a drunk and disorderly charge."

"Don't you talk to me like that, boy—"

Noah saw that one of the women had noticed them. Afraid she would head his way, he grabbed hold of Avery's arm, while reaching behind and opening the door. "Get in my office."

The old man's eyes bulged. "You locking me up?"

"Not if you come quietly." Noah spotted Roy's truck pulling to the curb, and he motioned for his deputy to meet him inside.

Avery started yapping before the door was closed. Noah tuned him out, glanced through the open blinds to see Roy approaching, and then turned his attention to the whirring groan of an incoming fax.

The machine was ancient, but they didn't use it much since they'd gotten the new computer, and Noah couldn't justify the expense of replacing it.

"What's up, boss?" Roy looked as if he'd just rolled out of bed with his spiky hair and wrinkled uniform shirt.

"Tuck it in," Noah said, snorting when Roy tried to suck in his sizable gut. "The shirt." Noah shifted a mislaid stack of papers from the corner of his desk to the top of the gunmetal-gray file cabinet. "Then take Avery home." He cut off the old man's protest with a stern glare before picking up the fax.

The silence lasted only a few seconds, but the arguing faded as the pair left the office, leaving Noah to concentrate on the fax sent from the Potter County Sheriff's Department. He knew Roland Moran, though not well, because Potter County was located south, clear down near the Idaho border. Sheriff Moran was old-school and had personally sent the fax.

Noah studied the piece of paper, seeing that he was one of four sheriffs who'd been notified that a pair of con artists might be headed north toward the Canadian border. Huh, grifters…that was something you didn't see every day. The man had a medium build, was in his mid-thirties with dark hair; the woman in her late twenties, brown hair, brown eyes, tall, attractive, the brains. Moran believed they were married but might be traveling separately.

Noah rubbed the tense spot in his right shoulder. Great, just what he needed. More trouble.

2

"MY BAGS?" ALANA PROMPTED when the cabbie pulled his atrocious ancient noisy sedan to the curb and just sat there, gazing out the windshield in apparent admiration of the cheap Halloween decorations that heralded Main Street.

"What? Oh, yeah, sure thing." Harvey popped the trunk, then made no move to get out and retrieve her luggage. He simply relaxed against the cracked vinyl upholstery, his impressive paunch testing the buttons of his plaid flannel shirt. "Easiest money I ever made. You gonna need a ride back to the airport later?"

"God, I hope not," she muttered, and dug in her purse for her wallet.

"What's that?" he asked, cupping a hand behind his ear.

"Your muffler," she said louder. "It needs replacing."

He just grinned and nodded.

Guess she was getting her own bag. At least it wasn't terrifically heavy. She sighed and passed him the fee she'd negotiated for him to drive her the hour and a half to Blackfoot Falls. To be fair, the man wasn't really a cab driver. She'd arrived at the tiny airport to find one car rental counter, and that was it. Since she didn't have a driver's license she supposed she was lucky to have gotten a ride from the rental agent's brother-in-law.

She climbed out of the car and yanked her bag from the trunk, setting it on its wheels before grabbing her carry-on and laptop, which she nested on top of the bag, anchoring everything securely to the pop-up handle. Normally, she was good at packing. But the last-minute trip and the mad dash to John F. Kennedy Airport to catch her plane had resulted in her purse ending up a catch-all that weighed heavily on her shoulder.

Alana watched Harvey make a U-turn, then sputter down the highway, tufts of disgusting black exhaust in his wake. She glanced around, hoping no one had noticed her arrival in the awful car, although she'd been careful to have him drop her off at the edge of town. He wasn't familiar with the Sundance, but she figured that as long as he got her to Blackfoot Falls, that was good enough. She just hoped there was someone around who could give her directions. The place looked deserted.

She tucked her hair behind her ear and smoothed down the front of her jacket while searching for signs of life. Farther down the street there were several cars parked in front of storefronts, but the place was ungodly quiet for…she checked her watch, did a quick calculation and set the Rolex back to four-thirty, local time.

It wasn't exactly the dinner hour, so where was everyone? Main Street looked to be about five blocks long, though surprisingly wide, with a small square of grassy semigreen in the middle, its centerpiece a huge tree with most of the leaves gone or faded to autumn-yellow. From the bare branches hung paper ghosts fluttering in the brisk breeze.

Not a single stop sign was in sight and definitely no traffic lights, even though there seemed to be a couple of residential side streets. Closest to her was a gas station, then a gun shop, and next to it a hardware store. Across the street was a video rental place and a pawn shop with a sign indicating the owner was gone for a week.

A number of stores stretched toward the far end of town, but Alana couldn't make out what they were except perhaps for another gas station. Other than a banner strung between two streetlights announcing the annual fall festival, and the ubiquitous Halloween decorations, the town was rather nondescript. She wouldn't be surprised if some of the shops had been abandoned, just like the old boarding house in back of her.

Her purse slipped off her shoulder as she noticed a woman and child carrying packages and walking toward a parked truck. As if a button had been pressed, the town seemed to spring to life. A pack of high-school-age kids started making themselves heard from down a long block. Three more pickups turned onto Main Street, one right behind the other, and a short, bowlegged man appeared on the sidewalk, headed in the opposite direction from her. Judging by his gait, Alana guessed he'd just left a bar.

Hell, she wouldn't mind a cosmo about now herself. She added her purse to the carefully stacked pile of bags, and then grabbed the suitcase handle and started walking, rolling her cargo behind her. By the time she'd made it a block, more people had shown up—a few in cars, but monster-size, dusty pickups appeared to be the vehicle of choice.

The action was clearly centered on the other side of town, so she hadn't received any curious looks yet. Although three women riding in a green sedan gave her a once-over as they passed. She watched them park and get out, and knew instantly by their tight, trendy clothes that they weren't locals. Had to be guests from one of the dude ranches in the area.

A few minutes later she got her first friendly wave from a man driving by in a white pickup with heavily tinted windows. Her pulse jumped when she saw the word *Sheriff* emblazoned in bold black letters on the door, but the driver wasn't the hottie she'd seen in the review pictures. Nevertheless, she watched him pull to the curb, get out and cross the street, then disappear inside the sheriff's office.

The wheels of her suitcase caught on a crack in the sidewalk, and she turned to give it a tug over the bulging concrete. The rough jerk upset the balance and she nearly lost the case with her laptop. Alana exhaled in relief, made sure stability had been restored, and headed for the green sedan. Maybe she'd be lucky enough to catch a ride with the blondes. Otherwise, she could call the Sundance, ask someone there to send a car for her. Or better yet, why not ask the sheriff for information?

She smiled at the idea. It was a perfectly reasonable thing for a tourist in a strange town to do. Even if said tourist could tell full well the town was too small to offer public transportation. What would be the harm? She'd get a nice close look and see for herself if the reviewers were right about him being all that. Not that she cared about small-town sheriffs, even if they did know how to fill out a uniform.

She picked up her pace, bumping along on the uneven sidewalk, watching more trucks coming down Main Street as if in a parade. They seemed to be headed to the same place, and though she wouldn't admit it, it was fun seeing all those cowboys pile out as each vehicle parked at the curb. Some of the men wore hats, some didn't. All were dressed in jeans and Western-cut shirts, and sported cowboy boots.

A few of them spotted her and gave her quick smiles, but they were more interested in the blondes artfully lounging near the sedan. Alana didn't take offense or give it a second thought. The women had dressed the part of tourists on the prowl, and she hadn't. Nor would she. She never flirted, acted coy or did any of those things. Even if she wanted to play the helpless, eye-batting, oh-aren't-you-a-big-strong-man game just for fun, she'd be really bad at it.

She crossed the street and saw the sign for the Watering Hole. Every time the door opened, country music blasted onto the sidewalk. Not only that, but the acrid smell of smoke was enough to choke a horse, and she was still half a block away. Guess she'd skip that place.

Too late, she realized she shouldn't have crossed yet. Groups of cowboys gathered outside the bar, smoking, talking or just plain gawking at the three women. Next door was a bank, with people coming and going, and in general, crowding the sidewalk.

The sheriff's office was only three doors down, so Alana stayed her course, weaving her way through the bottleneck.

"You staying at the Sundance?"

The gravelly voice sounded as if it came from behind her. She stopped and glanced over her shoulder, finding only an alley that seemed to lead to a dirt parking lot. The cowboys in front of the bar were talking among themselves; a couple of them were flirting with the women. No one paid her any attention.

"Over here."

She turned the other way and saw a tall, trim, older man with graying hair leaning against a post. His cowboy hat was pulled too low for her to see his eyes, and though the corners of his thin lips slowly lifted, it wasn't a particularly friendly smile.

"Yes," she said, noting that his boots were newer, expensive looking, and he was better dressed than the others. "Are you affiliated with the Sundance?"

His smirk turned a shade nasty. "Hell, no."

"Ah, then never mind."

"Sorry, miss…" He put out a weathered hand. "Didn't mean anything by that."

She stared at his fingers, brown and wrinkled from the sun, unsure what he expected from her.

After a long, awkward moment, he shoved both hands in his pockets. "You need help with anything? Directions, maybe?" He was showing lots of teeth now, suddenly a picture of charm, his voice silky smooth. "How about a drink?"

Her lips parted but her voice failed her. Dear God, this man could not be hitting on her. He was old enough to be her father. Helplessly, she cast a gaze at the cute young cowboys several yards away. They were focused on the blondes.

"No, thank you," she said finally, and flexed her fingers. They'd started to ache from pulling all her stuff. "I was just headed for the sheriff's office."

"Is there a problem?"

Her patience slipped, and she glanced pointedly at her watch. "I have to go. Thanks for the offer." She felt for the baggage handle, finding nothing but a brisk breeze that made her pull the lapels of her blazer together.

He lightly touched her arm. "You have a ride to the Sundance?"

She wouldn't go with him, that was for sure. "Excuse me, please."

A loud noise came from inside the bar—of glass shattering, someone yelling. It sounded as if an entire tray of drinks had crashed to the floor. Everyone's attention jerked toward the open door, and one of the cowboys hollered out something to Sheila, presumably a waitress, who responded with a salty curse.

Alana smiled and again reached behind her for her luggage handle. Again all she found was air. She jerked around.

And blinked.

What the hell? She made a complete circle. Her suitcase, her purse, her laptop...they were all gone. That couldn't be.

Her hand had been resting on the handle just a moment ago. This was crazy.

She spun around again, her heart nearly leaping out of her chest. A red truck was parked at the curb a couple feet away. She glanced in the bed, then checked the pickup parked close behind it. Panicked, she turned and looked up the alley, but there was nothing there.

"Dammit!"

This cannot be happening.

Frantic, she scanned the crowd, spotting the older man who'd talked to her walking in the direction she'd come from. "Sir, wait."

He ignored her and kept going, but then her voice barely carried above the music coming from the bar.

In fact, no one seemed to have heard her except a cowboy in a tan shirt, who swung her an inquiring look.

"That man," she said, pointing and hurrying toward the older gentleman, pushing her way through the crowd.

"Mr. Gunderson?" The cowboy frowned, but just when she thought he would ignore her, too, he cupped his hands around his mouth and shouted, "Hey, Gunderson."

The older man stopped, his posture erect and imposing, and he slowly turned around, his mouth a hard, thin line. He obviously wasn't someone who appreciated being summoned, and judging by the sudden tension radiating from the crowd, it didn't happen very often.

She felt a dozen pairs of curious eyes boring into her as she approached him. "My bags," she said. "They were right next to me while I was talking to you."

With his forefinger, he pushed back the brim of his hat. He had icy, piercing blue eyes, almost lifeless. He might've been an attractive man at one time, but he had a hard, cynical look that left her cold. "What about them?"

"They're gone. Did you see anything? Someone had to have come up behind me while we were talking...."

"Can't say that I did." He gave her a cool smile, then started to walk away.

She caught his arm. "You must have."

He peered purposefully at her restraining hand, shook it off and said, "I believe I just told you I didn't."

Was he being a bastard because she'd turned him down for a drink? She tensed her shoulders, tempted to hurl an accusation at him. If he hadn't seen anything, then maybe he was involved. "Really?"

His eyebrows rose slightly in challenge. "Really."

Damn him. "All right." She adjusted her lapels, keeping her gaze level with his, furious that her hands shook a little. But only because she was angry and helpless, and she really would've loved to knock this guy down a few pegs. "The name's Gunderson, right? I'll need it for the police report."

His mouth twitched into an oily smile. "Wallace Gunderson. Everyone in Blackfoot Falls knows me."

"I bet they do," she said sweetly, her eyes telling him a different story. "I imagine we'll be speaking again soon."

"Looking forward to it." He touched the brim of his hat and strolled across the street toward a big luxury SUV.

She muttered a strong, unflattering oath, and spun toward the sheriff's office.

"FOR GOD'S SAKE, ROY, THE guy's got over forty years on you. How the hell could you let him get away?" Noah yanked off his hat and pushed a hand through his hair in frustration. "Go make sure his truck is still there. Block it off if you have to."

"Cripes, boss, you know that old son of a gun is as wily as a fox staking out a henhouse. The darn varsity kids were out making a nuisance and, well, it could've happened to any of us."

"Just go. Avery shouldn't be driving."

His face flushed, the deputy swung open the door just as a woman was about to enter the office. She was tall, taller than Roy, who muttered an apology for nearly running her over.

She seemed unfazed as she slipped past him and met Noah's eyes. "Are you the sheriff?"

Damn it all to hell. Not another one. Those women from the Sundance didn't quit. This made three in two days, barging in, pretending she needed help with one thing or another. He'd begged Rachel to pull the silly reviews and pictures of him off her website, but she claimed they were good for business. He was gonna have to start working on his computer skills so he could hack in and do it himself.

"I'm Sheriff Calder." He settled his Stetson back on his head and discreetly got a look at her high heels. She had to reach six feet in those damn things. "What can I do for you?"

"I need to report a theft. It just happened. If you hurry you can probably still—"

He held up a hand. "Slow down."

Her brown eyes flared with temper, then narrowed. She pointed at the door, and not in a flirty way. Maybe she wasn't faking. "While you're taking your sweet time, someone is getting away with my things."

"Which would be?" he drawled, aware of his condescending tone, but she'd pissed him off. Taking his sweet time. Shit. And if this really was another theft...great. Just what he needed. The whole county was going to hell. "You'll have to describe what was stolen."

"Everything." She took a quick breath. "My luggage, laptop, purse...oh, God, my iPhone and wallet. Everything." She briefly closed her eyes, her long dark lashes sweeping the tops of her pale cheeks.

Noah took in her tailored, navy blue slacks, the expensive-looking blazer over a cream-colored blouse buttoned clear up to her throat. "You staying at the Sundance?"

"The what?" She gave her head a small shake. "The Sundance…yes, but I haven't checked in yet. I only just arrived in town."

She wasn't the typical Sundance guest. In fact, she didn't seem the type interested in staying at a dude ranch. More the high-powered, corner-office type used to getting what she wanted. The kind of domineering woman he'd quickly tired of in Chicago.

Her tongue darted out to moisten her pale pink lips, and she looked helplessly toward the door. By the time she turned to him again, she was back in control and glaring. "Why are you just standing there?"

"Look, I know you're upset, but I need more information. Why don't you have a seat?" He pulled out the worn black vinyl chair, and she eyed it as though it might bite her in the ass. "Have a cup of coffee while I take down some—"

"Listen, Sheriff, I'm not trying to tell you how to do your job, but—"

"Glad we understand each other." He sat in his own chair, behind his desk, and wasn't surprised when he met her eyes and found they were shooting daggers. "Where did the theft occur?"

She had a wide, generous mouth, which pulled thin with annoyance. "Near the bar," she said tightly.

"Were you inside?"

"No, I haven't been drinking," she said, her hoity-toity tone indicating she wouldn't step foot in a place like Sadie's.

"Ma'am, that wasn't the question. You could be hiding a flask under that jacket for all I care."

Her lips parted and she blinked. Then she startled him by grabbing her lapels and pulling open her blazer. "No flask, no nothing. That's my point. Everything. Is. Gone."

He wouldn't say "nothing." She had a nice rack. Noah cleared his throat, forced his gaze away from her breasts and back to the blank incident report he'd pulled out of his desk drawer. "Please describe for me what happened."

She heaved an annoyed sigh, and he couldn't help but glance surreptitiously at her chest again. Her blouse was made out of some kind of light silk and he saw that her bra was lacy.... "I was on my way here, rolling my luggage behind me, and just after I passed the bar—"

"Let's back up. You were on your way here, to my office?"

"Yes, I, um…" She flushed slightly, started to avert her gaze, then lifted her chin and looked at him dead-on. "I was coming to find out how I could get to the Sundance."

He frowned. She could've asked anyone for directions. "Why take your luggage out of the car?"

"I don't have a car. My ride left me at the edge of town."

That made no sense. "Why didn't you go straight to the Sundance?"

"What does that have to do with anything? I was robbed on your main street. You think I stole my own property?"

"No, ma'am, I don't. Just trying to get a clear picture." He offered her a conciliatory smile. It appeared she really was a victim, and he'd jumped to the wrong conclusion the moment she'd walked in. He'd gotten too used to the flimsy excuses the Sundance ladies had been throwing his way, trying to get his attention. "I haven't asked your name."

"Alana."

He waited for her last name.

"Look, Sheriff, I don't understand how this could've happened in broad daylight. I only looked away for a moment. In New York I wouldn't dare, but I figured in a small town like this…" She shrugged her slim shoulders, then slumped back with a sigh. "I understand it was my error. I should've been more careful."

"You're from New York, then?"

She hesitated, a flicker of alarm in her eyes that also made no sense. "Yes."

"I didn't catch your last name."

There it was again—that same wariness that had her shoulders tensing and straightening. After a long pause she said, "Richardson."

He slowly printed her name on the report, his cop's sixth sense on full alert. "How did you hear about the Sundance?"

She leaned forward. "Could it be someone playing a prank? I saw kids on the street earlier. Crime can't be much of a problem around here."

"You said you passed the Watering Hole?"

"That's right."

"Today is payday for most of the ranch hands. They were swarming outside the place, last I saw."

"Yes, there were quite a few cowboys hanging around."

Noah stopped writing and stared at her. "And that's where your things disappeared?"

She nodded. "An older gentleman stopped me, and it happened while I was talking to him. That's why I looked away."

"Did you get his name?"

"Gunderson."

Noah threw down his pen and leaned back. "What did Gunderson want with you?"

"He asked if I was staying at the Sundance. And then…" She made a face, appeared to reconsider what she'd been about to say. "I think he was just being nosy."

Noah reckoned she was probably right about that. Gunderson had always had it in for the McAllisters, but since they'd opened the dude ranch and were raking in money, he'd been especially ill-tempered. Their success meant they were unlikely to sell him that strip of land he wanted so badly.

"All those men out there…they would've noticed you," Noah said. "Someone had to have seen something."

"They were too busy to notice me," she said quietly.

"I doubt that."

Her startled expression and piercing stare made him re-examine his words. No, he hadn't said anything wrong, but maybe his tone could've been more professional. Hell, he hadn't consciously been thinking about what he'd glimpsed hiding behind that jacket…. But the notion that he might've blurred the line between the office and his personal feelings didn't sit well.

"Trust me," she said finally, her lips lifting in a faint smile. "There were three women who had the men's full attention."

Noah knew who she meant, but that didn't preclude the boys from checking her out. Yeah, the young cowhands in the area tended to go for that sort of flash, at least since the Sundance had been drawing in the ladies.

The woman facing him was different, one of those under-stated beauties. The longer you studied the high cheekbones, the nice skin, her generous mouth, the prettier she got. He knew most of those boys hanging out at Sadie's this afternoon, and they'd looked, all right. Noah could guarantee her that.

He picked up the pen again, his gaze catching on the fax sitting on the corner of his desk. Late twenties, tall, attrac-tive, brown hair, brown eyes.

His gaze shot back to Alana Richardson.

Well, hell.

3

BETWEEN THE POINTLESS questions and phone calls he'd answered since they started, the report was taking forever. And with each passing moment, life as she knew it was slipping away. The only compensation for this monumental hassle was that Alana liked the way the sheriff held his pen. Or more accurately, she liked his hands. Big-boned and tanned, with a light sprinkling of fine hair across the backs of his fingers. His uniform shirtsleeves were rolled back a couple times, displaying broad wrists and muscular forearms.

He stopped writing, and she lifted her gaze to find his mesmerizing blue-green eyes studying her face. Her breathing faltered for a second. The sheriff really was an extraordinarily good-looking man. Even better in person than in the photos.

She ordered herself to inhale slowly and focus on the problem. Oh, God, that's why she was so preoccupied with the sheriff. Every time she let herself consider the ramifications of losing her belongings, she thought she'd pass out. "Yes?"

"Other than Gunderson, did you talk to anyone?"

"No. I don't believe so."

He returned his gaze to the report and frowned slightly, pushing a hand through his longish, sun-streaked brown hair. It was thick, just like his lashes, which did nothing to distract from the rugged, outdoor look he had going on. Part of her job was to notice that sort of detail. Like how his biceps bunched and strained the material of his tan shirt as his hand slowly slid through his hair and then paused at the back of his neck.

No wonder those women had mentioned him in their reviews of the Sundance. Alana would sign him up for a print ad in a hot second. Or any kind of ad, for that matter. She couldn't imagine what she looked like at this point. Her poor limp hair needed work in the best of situations, and after that long plane ride, then Harvey's rust-mobile... Most of her makeup must have melted off by now. Hoping for a peek in her compact mirror, she glanced down for her purse.

With a start, she remembered it was gone. Along with her luggage and laptop and phone. That's why she was sitting here. She could feel the panic start to rise once more in her throat, in her chest. She lived her life on that phone, on that laptop. She barely knew anyone's phone number because they were all on speed dial or in her contact list. She hadn't spent twenty-four hours without access to the internet for longer than she cared to remember.

Not to mention her clothes or her makeup—which was worth a fortune. Her night cream alone cost a hundred dollars an ounce. She let out a small, pathetic whimper that surprised both of them.

The sheriff jerked his head up. "You all right?" He pushed away from his desk and got to his feet, his concerned gaze staying on her as he moved to a well-used coffeepot sitting on a metal filing cabinet. "I should've offered you something to drink. Water, coffee?"

What she needed was a good belt of Scotch. She wondered if he had a bottle stashed in his desk, because she sure didn't have cash to buy herself a drink. "Water," she said, nodding. "I could use some water."

She stared down at her watch. It was too late in New York

to call her bank and have money wired. Pam had left yesterday for Europe, so she'd be no help. But it would be all right.
Yes, it was an emergency, but Alana was good in emergencies.
She had her reservation at the Sundance, which took care of
a room and meals. They had her credit card information as
a guarantee, since Alana had known she'd be late, after having missed her flight last night....

"Here you go."

The nearness of his voice startled her. She looked up and
found him standing next to her, a bottle of water in his hand.
He was really tall, well over six feet. She'd noticed when she
first entered the office, which was something, considering her
state of mind. She managed a smile and accepted the water,
trying out one of those deep breathing tricks Pam was always
hounding her about. The one that was supposed to calm her
body. "Thank you."

He swung back around his desk, and she quickly inspected
his ass as he pulled out his chair. Impressive. Before he caught
her ogling him, she concentrated on uncapping the bottle,
then tilting it to her lips. She hadn't realized how thirsty she
was until she'd gulped down half the contents.

She used her fingertip to dab at the corner of her damp
mouth, then met his eyes. Wow, the man was intense. The
way he studied her was beginning to make her nervous. It
seemed out of place. She'd have expected that intensity in
Manhattan, but not ten miles north of nowhere.

His phone rang and he finally looked away, to answer the
call. "Sheriff Calder," he said into the receiver, his gaze coming back to her, briefly skimming the front of her blouse and
then resting on something over her left shoulder. "Anything?"
he asked the caller. "Right." His brows puckered in a slight
frown as he listened, and then he leaned way back in his chair,
his hand behind his head, making his biceps bunch again.

Alana didn't care if he knew she was staring at him. Once

she told him what she did for a living he'd understand that her interest was purely professional. Anyway, a man like him had to be used to the stares. So far, with his strong, square jaw and sexy eyes, his wide shoulders, broad chest and flat belly, she hadn't found a single flaw. The search was the only thing that was keeping her halfway sane.

It was a bit annoying, really. Unnerving, too, because he wasn't even her type. He lacked the polished sophistication that normally attracted her. Or if a man could get a reservation at Per Se on a Saturday night, that went a long way in piquing her interest.

All that crap aside, she'd do the sexy sheriff in a New York minute.

"What about Gunderson?" he asked the caller, and her gaze shot up to his face. He was watching her again, his eyes probing hers. "Okay. Check back."

"Was that about me?" she asked before he replaced the receiver. "Was anything recovered?"

He shook his head. "That was Deputy Tisdale who called earlier. He's been talking to the boys who were standing outside the Watering Hole. None of them saw anything."

She slumped back. At least Sheriff Calder took this seriously enough to have his deputy on the scene. "That seems impossible. How many people are walking around town rolling a big suitcase behind them?"

He raised his eyebrows, his dubious expression and head tilt difficult to interpret. It couldn't be that he didn't believe her…. Could it?

Alana straightened. "You can't possibly think I'm making this up."

"Didn't say that."

"Why?" She threw up her hands. "Why would I do such a thing?"

"No need to get upset." He reached for the phone again. "You have family you want to call?"

"Oh, God, no." She waved him off. "I remember something else—a loud noise came from the bar, like glass shattering. And there was an alley close to where I was talking to Mr. Gunderson... Did your deputy question him?"

"He hasn't been located yet." The sheriff slowly moved his hand away from the receiver. "What about this noise?"

"It sounded as if a waitress might have dropped a tray, and everyone turned to look toward the door. That's when someone could've grabbed my suitcase."

"By alley, you're referring to that narrow walkway between Sadie's and the bank?"

"I don't recall what was next door, but it led to a parking lot."

Nodding vaguely, he jotted something down at the bottom of the report.

Alana watched him, the enormity of her situation once again sinking in until she could barely breathe. She had no ID to travel, no money, not even a toothbrush, or a flat iron to straighten her hair. At least she had a place to sleep, she reminded herself before panic could take over. And she had her Rolex for collateral, though she imagined a place like the Sundance would cut her a break. Surely they'd help her arrange for toiletries or clothes or whatever else she needed until she could repay them.

"You know the people who run the Sundance, right?"

The sheriff looked up. "The McAllisters." He nodded. "Good folks."

"I was hoping..." She bit her lip. This was new territory for her. She wasn't in the habit of asking for help, or needing anyone. "I'm going to have to ask them for some assistance."

His eyes narrowed, the sudden distrust on his face quite insulting. "Such as?"

Alana cleared her throat. "I don't even have a damn tooth-brush."

"Ah. I can help out with that."

"Well, I'll need a few more things than a toothbrush and toothpaste. Look, I'd like to call the Sundance." She reached for the phone. "You mind?"

He hesitated, then lifted the receiver and punched in a number. When it became obvious he was going to play fa-cilitator, she leaned back, more than a little miffed. She hated being at other people's mercy.

She hadn't realized she'd sighed out loud until she met his probing gaze. He was wasting his time in this small town, she decided. With that cool, stoic stare he'd make an excel-lent big-city detective.

"Hey, Rachel," he said into the receiver, and his expression was suddenly transformed. Jesus, he was even better-looking when his features relaxed. "No, haven't seen him." He leaned back in his chair again and went into what she now consid-ered his telephone pose—one hand behind his head, biceps bulging, his broad chest tapering to his narrow waist. "Was he planning to stop by?"

That he was making small talk instead of focusing on her problem took a few seconds to register. Irritation broke through her admiration, and Alana sat up straight, tall and pissed. He seemed to get the drift, but instead of getting down to business, he held up his hand as he continued to chit-chat with the woman. Maybe Rachel was his girlfriend.

Finally, after a few more moments, Alana noisily cleared her throat.

Sheriff Calder's gaze touched on her face, then slid past her without hesitation.

Good-looking, yes, but he sure could be annoying.

"I'll be on the lookout for him," he said lazily. "Look, Rach, I got a small problem here with one of your guests.

What? No." His attention shot back to the window and his eyes narrowed in frustration. "But I'm warning you, that crap has to stop. Those gals…" He clamped his mouth shut as he resettled himself behind his desk and picked up the report.

Alana didn't try to hide her smile. She thought she saw a trace of color underscore his tanned skin, and suspected she knew what that part of the conversation was about. So the sheriff wasn't impressed with his fan club.

He focused on the piece of paper in front of him. "Alana Richardson. She hasn't checked in yet, but—" He frowned at Alana, repeated her name into the receiver, then fell silent.

She leaned forward. "What?"

"There's no reservation under that name."

"Yes, there is. I made it yesterday. I have a confirmation number right here…" No, she didn't. She had no purse, no nothing. "Dammit." She took a deep, shuddering breath and held out her hand. "May I speak with her?"

He listened intently for a minute, now holding up one finger instead of his hand, his impassive gaze flickering over her face. "She remembers now. You made a reservation for two, but that was for yesterday. You didn't show up so she sold the room to someone else."

"Because I missed my flight. But I gave her a credit card to guarantee the reservation." This was a nightmare. A complete and utter nightmare.

He held his palm over the phone. "Where's your companion?"

"What companion?"

"You booked the reservation for two."

"No, I didn't. She has me confused with someone else. I came alone. I'd like to talk to her." Alana still had her hand out, and through gritted teeth, added, "Please."

"That's okay," he said to Rachel. "I'll take care of it. I'm sure."

Alana watched him hang up the phone, her temper near boiling. "I asked to speak with her."

"I'm sorry, in the middle of the conversation something came up on her end. But she told me that she's completely booked. She has no rooms at all."

"What am I supposed to do? Sleep in the alley?"

He smiled. "I don't think that'll be necessary."

"You think this is funny, Sheriff?"

"No, ma'am, I don't." He didn't seem the slightest bit chastened as he pushed away from the desk and started to stand. But the office door opened, and he stayed right where he was.

Alana turned to see who'd just wiped the faint smirk off his face. Two of the blondes she'd seen earlier walked in, very perky blondes in their early twenties. They were certainly full of smiles for the sheriff.

No cheery welcome from him, Alana noticed when she turned back to follow his reaction.

His mouth was a narrow line, thin and unsmiling. "Yes, ladies, what can I do for you?"

"We were hoping you'd be getting off work about now," one of them said. "Doesn't Roy or Gus have the second shift?"

He scrubbed a hand over his face and sighed. "I'm still on duty."

"Oh." She sounded disappointed. "When do you get off, Noah?"

His gaze flickered to Alana, who wouldn't give up her front-row seat for anything. She didn't even turn to check out the woman who was talking. Much more informative to watch him trying not to squirm. Oh, he was good at hiding his reaction, but Alana had no doubt he was not happy with the attention.

"Is there sheriff's business I can help you with, ma'am?" he asked evenly, getting up and grabbing his hat off the scarred wooden table that seemed to serve as a credenza.

"I told you already, you can call me Cindy," she said with a hint of frustration in her voice.

Alana pressed her lips together and watched him lazily set the Stetson on his head. She was pretty sure his actions were meant as a dismissal, but the way he looked settling that cowboy hat on his head was not going to get any woman with a pulse to turn around and leave.

While his attention was directed elsewhere, Alana studied his fancy belt buckle and wondered if he'd won it in a rodeo competition. That would make him very popular in the New York print market. She could see him as the face of one of Ralph Lauren's colognes. She knew next to nothing about real rodeos or cowboys, only what she'd gleaned from movies she'd watched as a kid. These days, who had time for movies? Certainly not her, though she knew how to appreciate a fine male specimen. But then, that was a trait learned over years of dealing with models and actors. Alana was highly aware that the package had little to do with the contents.

And his package was exceptional. The way the worn denim caressed his lean hips and hard-looking thighs brought her back to the idea that he'd spent considerable time sitting astride a horse. She'd like to see that, she decided—him riding a large, powerful stallion. She didn't have the faintest idea why the image suddenly appealed to her. The whole fleeting fantasy of a hot vacation fling was crazy.

She should be furious with the man for his attitude, his cavalier approach to the theft. The last thing on her mind should be his physique or his discomfort over the attention. And what the hell had happened to her reservation? This whole trip was the worst idea in the history of ideas, and all Alana wanted was to get back on a plane and go home.

But first, she needed her purse and her luggage, because without her ID, she wasn't going anywhere. "Can we finish this?" she asked, her patience thinning as he strolled past her toward the other two women.

He went to the door, opened it. "Ladies, if there's nothing else, I have business to attend to."

The blondes exchanged defeated glances. "If you change your mind we'll be at the Watering Hole," Cindy said and led her disappointed friend outside.

He gave Alana a dry look as he returned to his desk and pulled out his middle drawer.

"I read the reviews for the Sundance," she said, knowing it would bother him. "You're quite popular."

He concentrated on whatever he was looking for, but she could see irritation deepen into brackets at the corners of his mouth. "Ready?"

She sprang up. "Where are we going?"

"To get you settled in."

"Thank you," she said, heading for the door, and feeling no guilt for having baited him. He had all the power, and that wasn't something she could easily accept. She'd needed to even things up a bit. Show him she could be indifferent to his charms and that she wasn't a helpless victim. "I appreciate this, and I'll certainly reimburse your office for any costs—"

"Not that way."

She hesitated, turned, her gaze darting to the key he held in his hand.

He motioned with his chin toward the back of the office, where a short hall led to another door. A bathroom? Not that she couldn't use one about now, but she'd prefer to purchase some toiletries first. Or more likely, his truck was parked out back....

Alana pulled her blazer more snugly around herself, mostly because she needed something to do with her hands. She was used to carrying a purse or her phone, and she couldn't shake the odd feeling of having nothing to hold on to.

The sheriff gestured for her to precede him down the hall. It was a small space and she had to squeeze by him. Her arm brushed his chest, and her hip touched God-knew-what, but the brief contact was enough to quicken her pulse, which was unnerving for a number of reasons. Her appraisal of the sheriff had been strictly professional.

She grabbed the doorknob, couldn't budge it, then felt him reach around her.

"It's not locked," he said, his face so close that his warm breath tickled her ear. "It just sticks." He jiggled the knob, then pushed the door open.

For a long, absurd moment she hesitated. He'd lightly touched the small of her back, or at least she thought she felt the pressure of his hand, and she had a bit of trouble maintaining her balance. Probably dehydrated, she reasoned, or weak from hunger. Had she eaten today? Nope, just black coffee on the plane. With as much traveling as she'd done one would think she wouldn't still have a nervous stomach every time she flew.

"Ms. Richardson?"

"What?" Startled, she turned too quickly and had to hold on to the wall for support.

"Are you okay?"

"I'm fine."

This time there was no doubt that he'd pressed a palm to her back. "Look at me," he said, catching her chin and bringing her face around to his. Eyes shaded with concern, he looked deep into hers before moving on to study her face. "You look pale."

"It's nothing." She jerked her chin away. "I've had a long day. It's not easy getting from New York to Montana at the last minute."

"You were in a hurry?" He didn't look concerned now, just appeared oddly invested in her answer.

"I suppose you could say that." She smiled wryly, wondering how her mother had reacted to the cryptic message she had left her. Alana had even gone so far as to tell her housekeeper and doorman she'd be in the Caribbean in case her mother contacted them. Eleanor would be at wit's end by now, analyzing how she'd lost control of her daughter. "I'd prefer you call me Alana."

"All right." His mouth curved slightly. "Noah is okay with me."

His stare was surprisingly captivating, and she forced herself to turn away before she made a fool of herself. God forbid she start acting like one of his groupies. She pushed the door open the rest of the way. Three steps over the threshold, she froze.

The entire room consisted of two jail cells, each one furnished with nothing more than a cot and a toilet.

4

WHEN SHE WOULDN'T MOVE, NOAH sidestepped her and unlocked the cell with the small barred window and the newer
cot. He did feel a twinge of guilt for coldcocking her. For one
thing, she might be innocent, a tourist in the wrong place at
the wrong time, just as she'd claimed. If that proved to be
the case, he'd still feel bad for the McAllisters. Rachel had
worked hard to build the dude ranch business, and if news of
this incident got out, people might not be so anxious to come
to Blackfoot Falls.

The other thing was, Alana really had looked pale a minute ago. But then if she was Sheriff Moran's suspect and had
been double-crossed by her partner, yeah, she might be feeling a little helpless and panicked.

Or she was playing Noah like a fiddle. He couldn't take
that chance. He hadn't had a lot of personal experience with
grifters, but he'd heard plenty of stories. Most of them centered around a brazen act, something so crazy no one ever
thought to question it. Like, say, turning to the town sheriff
for help then waiting for the right moment to escape across
the border.

Either way, whether she was innocent or on the make, he
had to deal with facts, which defied the likelihood that she'd

been robbed in broad daylight in front of half a dozen cowboys who hadn't seen a thing. True, the recent thefts had to be considered, but they fell into a different category, with a different M.O. The victimology was wrong.

It could have been the varsity team, but they toed the line under the new coach. And then, too, someone could be yanking Noah's chain because of all the attention he'd been getting from the Sundance female guests. Not Cole or Jesse. They knew better. But he wouldn't put it past Trace to send someone like Alana into his office with some cockamamie story just to get a rise out of him.

He stood back, holding the cell door open, and eyed the disbelief on her face. If she was faking her appalled reaction, she was a damn good actress, he'd give her that.

"You're kidding." She slowly turned her head and regarded him, wide-eyed with shock. "Tell me you're kidding."

"You'll have clean sheets."

She covered her mouth with her hand, then quickly removed it and stiffened her spine. "I am not staying in that… that—" She shuddered. "Oh, my God. This is seriously, seriously insane. I'm already a victim and you want to further victimize me by sticking me in a jail cell?"

"No, ma'am. The way I see it, I'm offering you a safe place to sleep."

She made a small, exasperated sound of distress.

"The meals aren't bad, either. Marge at the diner will bring over breakfast and supper."

"Okay," Alana said with forced calmness, her brown eyes blazing mad. "If this is supposed to be a joke, it's not funny in the least."

"You tell me. Is this a joke? Did Trace put you up to this?"

She blinked, rubbing her left temple. "Who the hell is Trace?"

Noah sighed. Maybe that had been reaching too far. She

hadn't been flirty or silly like the other women staying at
the Sundance.

"I apologize. It's just that—" He cleared his throat. "You
did seem to be enjoying that little scene back there," he said,
glancing toward the office.

"Oh." A small, guilty smile curved her generous mouth.
"Well, yes, you're right. I did." Her gaze returned to the jail
cell. "Come on, this is overkill."

Overkill? Took him a second. "This isn't payback. I honestly figured this might be a good solution." He shrugged.
"At least for tonight."

Her lips parted and she stared at him with those pretty
brown eyes. "I have money. I do. Isn't there a hotel in town?"

He shook his head.

"I'd like to speak to that woman at the Sundance," Alana
insisted. "I'm sure we can come to some arrangement. I'll
sleep on a couch if I have to."

Damn, he couldn't let her talk to Rachel. The truth was,
Rachel had offered to scare up a room for her in the family wing. Not knowing if this woman was a criminal or not,
Noah couldn't unleash her on the McAllisters. No, better he
keep an eye on her until he sorted out her identity. When all
was said and done, it was mighty suspicious that she wouldn't
call family or a friend.

"I'll tell you what," he said, closing the cell door. "I live
around the corner and I have a spare room."

She stared at him as if he'd asked her to submit to a strip
search. "You're suggesting I stay with *you.*"

"That's right." Already, he was regretting the offer. Install-
ing her at his house made sense, though. He could keep an
eye on her, and if she truly was a victim, the least he could
do was give her a safe place to sleep. "There's not much to
the guest room, but it has a double bed with a new mattress.
Nothing else in there, but then you don't have any luggage."

She nibbled at her lower lip. "Wouldn't people talk?"

Unprepared for that reaction, Noah laughed out loud.

Alana glared at him. "Just because I don't look like Cindy doesn't mean people wouldn't gossip behind your back."

He shook his head. She'd surprised him again. "I didn't peg you for someone who gave a crap about what people thought."

"Believe me, I don't." She looked as if she meant it. In fact, she looked as if it would take a sizable quake to rattle her.

He knew the type. She reminded him of a woman he'd dated in Chicago. Kara was a defense lawyer, a real ball-buster who'd ended up driving him nuts with her need for perfection, eye always on the prize, never taking a moment to watch the grass grow. That was one of the reasons he was having trouble buying that Alana would choose to go to a dude ranch. "Let's get you settled in, and then we can grab supper at Marge's. How does that sound?"

"A toothbrush sounds better."

"Just so happens I have a spare at home." He motioned for her to go first down the hall.

"I bet you do," she muttered under her breath as she strode past him.

He smiled, guessing she hadn't meant to be overheard. He followed her but stayed far enough behind to enjoy the view. The hip-length jacket got in the way, but she had nice long legs even without the heels.

"I'm going to need a few other things," she said over her shoulder. "I hope your office has some petty cash. Naturally, we'll keep a record of my expenditures, and like I said earlier, I'll reimburse you for everything."

They got to the outer office and she abruptly spun to face him. Caught by surprise, he nearly rammed into her. His arms shot out, and he caught her shoulders when she teetered toward him.

"Oh, sorry." She placed a palm on his chest and steadied herself.

"Are you dizzy?"

"No, not at all." She lowered her hand.

He didn't let go. Her shoulders were slimmer than he'd expected, more fragile under the heavy tweed blazer. He wanted to make sure she didn't start reeling. "That's the second time you've lost your balance. Maybe we ought to stop by the clinic."

She adamantly shook her head, loosening the hair that had been tucked behind her ears, until it swung freely around her heart-shaped face. "If you have a piece of hard candy, that might help. I think it's low blood sugar."

"Are you diabetic?"

"No, I just haven't eaten in a while."

"We'll have to take care of that right away." He slipped an arm around her shoulders and guided her back to the chair.

"Really, I'm okay." Her laugh was short, nervous, maybe embarrassed. She refused to sit. "I'd rather go pick up some toiletries and get to your house."

He knew Roy kept candy in his desk because his wife didn't allow it in their home. Noah found a hard butterscotch and a few Hershey kisses in the deputy's top drawer. "Here you go."

She took the butterscotch from his open palm. "I don't even care if it's stale."

He chuckled. "I doubt Roy leaves sweets around long enough."

"Thank him for me." She bowed her head and delicately peeled open the wrapper with trembling fingers.

In spite of himself, Noah felt his chest tighten with sympathy. He again urged her to sit down, and then got a fresh bottle of water out of the minifridge. He uncapped the bottle before setting it on the desk in front of her, and watched her slip the butterscotch into her mouth.

The tip of her tongue swiped at her lower lip, and his whole body tensed for a moment. He rolled a shoulder and glanced away. Maybe he ought to sit down, too. She might need a minute. He sure did. He felt better once he'd put his desk between them.

Her gaze went to his chest, then drifted up to meet his. "I'm being a real pain in the ass, aren't I?"

"Not your fault. Hope you don't hold what happened against the Sundance." He kept his eyes steady on hers. "The McAllisters are fine folks."

"Of course I wouldn't hold any of this against them. Good God, I shouldn't have let go of the suitcase handle. I'm a New Yorker. I know better."

"You don't have an accent."

Her sudden smile caught him off guard. She was plenty attractive, but when her lips tilted up like that she could throw a man off his game. "Neither do you, Sheriff."

"Reckon I deserved that."

"I knew what you meant." Her smile fading, she idly tugged at her blouse collar, then unfastened the top button. "I went to prep school in Connecticut. No common accents allowed. And if the headmistress hadn't put her foot down, Eleanor would have." Alana slid the second button free and took a deep breath. "Are we leaving soon? Otherwise I think I'll take off my jacket. It's a bit warm in here."

He wouldn't mind seeing what she looked like under that heavy tweed.... Hell, what was wrong with him? "How are you feeling? Think you could walk to my truck at the curb?"

Her cheeks were slightly flushed. "We're going straight to the store, aren't we?"

"If we are, better you sip some water and wait to give that sugar a chance to work."

Moistening her lips, she nodded, then started to reach for the bottle. She stopped and shrugged out of her jacket. "I'm too warm."

Noah stared at her thrusting breasts, realized what he was doing, and forced his gaze out the window. "Why haven't you eaten?"

She hesitated, long enough that her apparent reluctance to answer drew his attention back to her. "I was rushed." She grabbed the water bottle, looked away and gulped greedily.

He got the impression she didn't want to be pressed. "In a hurry to get out of the city?"

"Sort of." She dabbed at her mouth and sighed. "I feel better already. I thought it would be cooler here this time of year."

"Oh, it's plenty cool at this altitude and this far north, especially after the sun sets. Might be a little stuffy because I'd just closed everything up before you walked in. Ever been to Montana before?"

She gave him a small, rueful smile. "No. I haven't spent a lot of time outside of the two coasts."

Well, if she was one of the pair who'd pulled off those scams in Potter County, she was a damn fine actress. Or maybe Noah plain ol' wanted to believe her. That wasn't good. He adjusted his hat and got to his feet. "Think you're ready?" he asked gruffly.

She blinked at him, then arranged her jacket over her arm. Her eyes watchful and confused, she slowly got up.

God, he was an ass. "We can wait if you need to."

Her chin lifted with determination. "I'm fine. Thank you."

He nodded, then walked ahead of her to get the door. Standing aside, holding it open while she crossed the threshold, he recalled something odd she'd said earlier. "By the way, who's Cindy?"

WHEN ALANA LEARNED THAT HIS house sat on a side road half a block down, and that he normally left his truck in front of the office when he went home, she insisted they walk, as well. The crisp air felt good, almost too chilly, but she'd scared herself back in his office.

They were about to walk past the Watering Hole when Noah touched her arm and indicated they should cross the street. "Isn't this jaywalking?" she asked as they stepped off the curb.

A faint smile tugged at his mouth. "Guess you are feeling better."

After they got to the other side, she stopped and looked back. "Oh, did you want to duck in and say hi to Cindy and her friend?"

Noah practically glowered at her. "This is how you repay my hospitality."

She laughed and hurried to catch up with his new, quicker pace. "Come on, that was impossible to resist."

"You can always sleep in the jail." He rolled down one sleeve and then went to work on the other.

"Speaking of jail, what are you planning to do about Mr. Gunderson and my stolen luggage?"

He nodded thoughtfully. "The deputies and I will question everyone who could have been anywhere near the Watering Hole. Someone had to have seen something."

"Gunderson certainly did."

"I'll be talking to him myself."

"When?"

That brought a scowl to the sheriff's face, but she didn't care. While it was fine that he'd lend her a toothbrush, she wanted her own.

"Soon," he said, as he continued their walk.

They turned on a short side street and headed up the slight

incline. Nothing more was said until he stopped her with a gentle hand on her arm.

"Here we are."

She turned her head to see a small blue house with white trim and a matching picket fence. "This is yours?"

"It belongs to the county." He opened the gate. "Comes with the job."

"It's cute."

He grunted. "Yeah."

"No, I'm serious."

"I know," he said flatly, and motioned for her to get going.

She passed through the open gate, but took her time following the walkway that wound toward the red front door, trying to imagine the bordering beds filled with bright-colored flowers. There were remnants of dead daisies and carnations. A few pink and yellow mums were still in decent shape.

She stopped at the porch and turned for a last look. "Did you plant these flower beds yourself?"

"No." He almost sounded insulted.

"Real men do plant flowers," she said.

"Maybe." He took the four steps up to the covered porch, two at a time. "This one doesn't." He opened both the screen and wooden doors, neither of which were locked. "The ladies from the betterment committee tend to the yard."

"Comes with the job, too?"

"I've never put it to the test, but I doubt I'd have any say."

"A smart man knows when to back off."

"Amen." He smiled, replacing the last of her discomfort with a vivid awareness of how much she wanted to trace the groove in his cheek with her fingertip.

She kept her hands to herself and walked past him into the house. Despite the awkward situation, she liked Noah, especially when he loosened up. It would've been such a shame if he was pretty but had no personality.

Although it was still light out, the sun was setting on the west side of the house and most of the living room was cast in shadow. He flipped a switch and two brass lamps, one sitting on each side of the tan leather couch, produced a soft yellow glow. The floor was old and wooden; the walls painted a pale eggshell. The only color that livened up the place was from a pair of braided rugs, one in front of the couch and the other before the stone fireplace that spanned most of the wall.

"I haven't done much with the place yet," he murmured, flipping on a hall switch. "As you can see."

"How long have you lived here?"

He took off his hat and rubbed his hair, wincing a little. "A while. The kitchen is over there." He motioned vaguely past an oak table with four chairs and matching china hutch. "Both the fridge and pantry are stocked with the basics. I'll show you the guest room."

He led the way, which she appreciated, since it would take a minute for her to get tired of admiring his backside and long lean legs. His boots sported an inch heel, but not because he needed the boost. "How tall are you?" The words were out of her mouth before she knew what she was going to say.

Noah stopped and glanced at her with a faint expression of amusement. "Six-four." Then he looked at her feet. "You're pretty tall yourself. Even without those heels."

"I like being tall."

"Good thing." He smiled, probably because she'd sounded defensive, though why she had was a mystery to her. "I hope the bed is comfortable enough for you."

She followed his gaze into the small bedroom with the same eggshell-colored walls. The floor was carpeted in dark beige, and the blue gingham curtains looked homemade, as did the navy-and-brown patchwork quilt covering the double bed.

"It's better than the cell you tried to stick me in." Wishing she had her luggage with her, Alana sighed. "My life is in that purse."

"You should cancel your credit cards." He dug in his pocket. "Use my phone."

She stared at the black cell phone in his hand, trying to remember which cards were in her wallet. What a nightmare. Alana prided herself on being in control, on top of every aspect of her life. No matter how many balls were in the air, she caught each and every one. In her position at Giles and Reese Advertising, she was both envied and feared. She liked being that person. She'd actively cultivated the image of superwoman, of someone to be reckoned with. Right now she felt like a damn child.

"Thanks," she said, accepting the phone with all the enthusiasm of someone facing a trip to the dentist. Feeling foolish she could handle—not with total aplomb, but she could suck it up. What she couldn't handle was the stupid emotion snowballing in her chest. Where the hell was that coming from? Other than being tired and hungry and hating feeling helpless…

"Look." He touched her arm. "You need food and probably a stiff drink."

"Maybe more than the food," she murmured, her voice whisper-thin and embarrassingly shaky. She cleared her throat, tried again. "You wouldn't happen to have phone numbers for American Express and Visa, would you?"

He took her jacket from over her arm and tossed it on the bed. Then he put his hands on her shoulders, propelled her out of the room and down the hall toward the living room.

"What are you doing?" She tried to turn around, but he held firmly until he got her to the couch.

"Sit."

"I thought—"

He wasn't rough, but he made sure her ass hit the seat. "I'm gonna scramble a couple of eggs and make toast, just so you have something in your stomach. I'll even get you that whiskey I promised." He reached into his breast pocket, pulled out a small notebook, tore off a page and gave it to her with a pen. "Call directory assistance, get the numbers you need. Make your calls."

"What about picking up some toiletries?"

"Eat first."

Alana gave orders; she rarely took them. His bossiness was enough to put the bone back in her spine. "I don't like my eggs scrambled."

Noah had already started for the kitchen. He slowly turned to meet her gaze. "Alana?"

"What?"

"You're welcome," he said, and winked.

5

NOAH PULLED A COUPLE T-SHIRTS out of his dresser drawer. The white one was still in the package, and the black long-sleeve he'd worn once, but it was freshly laundered. He figured he'd let her decide if she wanted to wear either one to sleep in or while she was hanging around the house.

It was only six-fifty, but Abe's Variety had closed early this evening because Abe had to drive to Billings to pick up more Halloween decorations. Fall and winter retail hours were always hit-and-miss in Blackfoot Falls. The Watering Hole and Marge's Diner were the only establishments anyone could count on being open past dark.

"Knock knock."

He looked up.

Alana stood at his open bedroom door. Or rather, she was lounging against the door frame, her head tilted at a fetching angle, her hair tousled around her face. He'd be willing to swear on a stack of Bibles he hadn't meant to get her tipsy. But with so little food in her belly, he supposed he should've put the bottle away after her second glass of whiskey.

"It's for you," she said, holding out his cell phone, and then primly covered a yawn.

He promptly crossed the room to take the device. The ring

must've woken her. She'd been nodding off when he left her on the couch. "Sheriff Calder." He went back for the T-shirts and handed them to her. "Yeah, Roy. She's staying with me."

Noah took in her confused frown as she shook out the black shirt, and she looked so cute with her nose wrinkled that he momentarily lost track of the conversation. When the deputy asked him what the hell was going on, he said, "Let me get back to you, and let Cole know I'll call him later."

"What's this?" she asked, her brown eyes sleepy and unfocused.

He slipped the cell phone into his breast pocket. "Something to sleep in until we get to the store tomorrow."

"I thought we were going today."

"It's too late. They're closed."

She studied her watch. "Oh my, it's almost eight. I must've fallen asleep."

"Only for a few minutes. We're on mountain time here, which is seven." Interesting that her watch wasn't set on East Coast or Montana time. Either one could've supported her story that she was a tourist who'd flown in earlier today.

"Oh, I turned it back when I arrived here. I don't know why I set it on Central Time." She slipped the gold watch off her slim wrist and squinted at the face as she fumbled with trying to change the time.

"Here." He took the Rolex from her, gauged the heaviness in his hand. Solid gold; the trademark crown was in the right spot; the second hand didn't hesitate. It was the real thing, and set an hour ahead. He changed the time and returned the watch to her.

"Thank you." She smiled groggily and pressed the black shirt to her cheek. "It's soft. Are these yours?"

The innocent gesture of her rubbing her cheek against the cotton did something funny to the inside of his chest. Maybe because with her guard down and the sleepiness in her eyes she seemed different, softer, sexier. It had nothing to do with the way her blouse gaped, allowing him a glimpse of pink lace and pale skin. Sure, he'd looked, by accident and only for a second.

"Yeah, the white one is brand-new," he said unnecessarily, indicating the package. "The other is freshly laundered." He moved closer to her and the door, hoping she'd get the hint and leave his bedroom.

She stayed put, her head and shoulder supported by the door frame, and smiled dazedly. "You're not just gorgeous, you can be very nice when you want to."

Noah exhaled sharply, gave her a small tap and pointed down the hall. "You still hungry? Marge's will be open for another hour."

Straightening, Alana seemed to regain her senses. "No, the eggs and toast were perfect. What about you? Because we could go out if you want, or I could wait here...."

"I'm good." He herded her toward the living room, unsure why her standing at his bedroom door bothered him. Maybe because he never brought women home with him. Salina County seemed to shrink to the size of an acorn when it came to folks' noses being everywhere, even behind closed doors.

When he got the itch for some female companionship, he headed over to Twin Creek Crossing in the next county. Tanya, the afternoon waitress at Sully's, was pretty and willing and never expected more than dinner, some conversation and a warm body.

Alana stopped short and pointed. "That's the bathroom."

He nodded. "The house is old so there's only one." It was also tiny and the turquoise walls damn near gave him a headache. How many times had he told himself he'd slap on a coat of neutral paint? "I laid out fresh towels for you."

"Thanks. I'd love a shower. Unless you need to..." She gestured awkwardly.

"Go ahead." He flipped the light switch on for her. "I meant to ask—do you have a problem with dogs?"

"Me? No, I like dogs. As long as they don't slobber all over me."

"Dax is out back. I bring him in at night." Noah smiled as he walked off. "I'll remind him not to slobber."

"Cute," she said drily, and then closed the bathroom door.

He waited until he heard the shower start, and then took out his cell phone. After a discussion with Roy about the investigation, and a warning to keep his mouth shut about Alana, Noah called Cole McAllister.

"Figured I wouldn't hear from you for a week," Cole said by way of greeting.

"I knew you'd give me shit." Noah decided he was off duty, and grabbed a glass from the kitchen cupboard, along with the bottle of whiskey. "What did Roy tell you?"

"You have a hostage situation."

"Yeah, me." He poured himself two fingers worth, put the bottle away and headed for the back door, while Cole got in a couple digs. Noah supposed he deserved it, after all the crap he'd given Cole for hooking up with a Sundance guest two months ago and then chasing her all the way to California. "You done?"

"Until I think of something else." Cole chuckled. "What's going on? Roy wasn't making much sense."

Noah pushed open the screen door. Roy shouldn't have said anything about county business, but he knew Cole and Jesse McAllister were like brothers to Noah, and Roy tended to be looser lipped around them. Still, they'd have to be careful about accusing Alana of anything.

"What I tell you has to stay between you and me," Noah said. "Of course you can say something to Jesse if the need arises, but nothing to Rachel."

"All right."

Dax had apparently heard his voice and came bounding out of the little house Noah had built for the border collie mix. "Easy, boy." Noah almost lost his drink. "Wait a second," he told Cole, and set the glass on the redwood picnic table he never used. "Sorry, I needed a free hand." He made sure the bathroom light was still on before he explained the whole story to his friend.

"It's a hell of a coincidence, her showing up like that," Cole said.

"Yeah. And hard to believe nobody saw her luggage being lifted or that someone would be that bold." Noah stroked Dax's head. "I don't know...I got a weird feeling about her."

"Gotta go with your gut."

"Yep, that's what I'm doing. The thing is, I can't have Rachel offering to put her up." Noah went on to explain, while he sipped his whiskey and threw a ball for Dax until the bathroom light went off.

Then he disconnected and took the mutt through the back door with him. He stopped in the kitchen, washed out his glass and left it on the rack to dry.

Dax obviously knew they had a visitor, and took off around the corner. Noah called him back, heard his short bark, then heard Alana say, "Oh, aren't you a handsome boy."

Noah left the kitchen and found her in the living room bent on one knee, petting Dax, who seemed determined to lick her chin. She seemed equally resolute in not letting him, straining backward until he'd nearly knocked her over.

She wore Noah's long-sleeved black T-shirt, and no pants. His heart lurched. He hadn't even considered digging up a pair of sweats, though come to think of it, he wasn't sure he owned any. All he ever wore were jeans.

"Dax, come here."

She gamely said, "He's fine." Even as the dog took a sloppy swipe at her averted chin.

"Dax," Noah said sternly. "Come."

The mournful mutt's tail stopped wagging and he dutifully reported to Noah's side.

She was all legs…smooth, toned legs. While tugging at the hem of the shirt, Alana braced a palm on the wall and slowly drew herself up. The fabric ended high on her thigh.

Noah realized he should've offered her a hand, but he was so distracted by the expanse of creamy skin that he didn't trust himself. And here she was worried about Dax slobbering all over her.

"I see the shirt fits," Noah muttered lamely, sucking in a breath when he noticed something else. No bra. Nice high, full breasts. Oh, hell.

"Yes, thanks." She glanced down. "It's even longer than I expected."

Not long enough. Or thick enough. Not for his peace of mind. He backed up, massaged the tense muscle at the side of his neck. Tried everything in his power to keep his eyes above her shoulders. "I just remembered I might have a pair of flannel sleep pants."

She folded her arms across her breasts, fairly nonchalant about her sudden shift in position, but he had a feeling she was uncomfortable. He just hoped it had nothing to do with his reaction. "I wouldn't turn them down," she said. "It's a bit cool."

"I'll go check." He couldn't wait to escape to his bedroom before she saw that he was getting hard. Maybe she already had, though he didn't think so. He'd purposely bent over to pet Dax.

Hell, he was too old for his cock to be surprising him like that. He dug deep in his lower dresser drawer and came up empty. When it was warm he slept in boxers, and during the colder months he practically lived in long johns. She'd have to be desperate for him to offer her a pair of those things. They were old and needed replacing.

But he remembered a Christmas gift that he'd never worn, and kept rooting around until he found it on his closet shelf still in the box. Blue-and-green-plaid sleep pants, medium-weight wool with a drawstring waist, or so advertised. They'd cover her legs. That would do both of them a world of good.

Thinking about where the T-shirt hem hit her midthigh, exposing those sleek toned legs, had him stopping in the bathroom on the way back. He remembered her hard nipples poking at the soft thin cotton, and splashed ice-cold water on his face. God help him, he supposed it could've been worse had she chosen the white shirt.

He waited until he felt reasonably under control and then joined her in the living room. She was sitting on the couch, her legs curled up under her while she cooed in a soft, melodic voice to Dax. The mutt's admiring gaze was planted on her face and didn't so much as waver with Noah's approach.

"You'll probably have to roll them up." He started to hand her the box, but then pulled the package out and shrugged. "A Christmas present from my mom."

"I see it was a big hit."

Noah smiled wryly, noting with both relief and regret that she'd taken the brown afghan from the back of the couch and wrapped it around her shoulders. "You have a fan."

She grinned at Dax. "I told him I'd ask you if it was okay to give him a treat."

The mutt's ears perked up.

"Oops. Guess I should've spelled it."

"He has quite a vocabulary, especially when he wants something." Noah made himself comfortable on the recliner. "Now you've gotta come through. The Milk-Bone jar's on the kitchen counter."

She glanced in that direction. "Do you suppose he'll forgive me if I go put these bottoms on first?"

"What do you think?"

Alana narrowed her eyes at Dax, whose gaze remained locked on her face. "I think he has a long memory, something I'd do well to remember."

"You're quick."

"Apparently, not quick enough." She carefully swung her feet to the floor, making sure the afghan was strategically placed in front of her.

Noah was a bastard for making her get up. He could've brought her the doggie treat, but he wanted another look at those legs before she covered them with that ugly blue plaid thing. Totally unprofessional of him, but he figured he could've been a worse bastard by not giving her the pants at all.

"Are you still on duty?" she asked, heading to the kitchen with Dax close on her heels.

Damn. The traitorous mutt blocked a good part of Noah's view. "No. Why?"

"You're still wearing your uniform shirt." She disappeared into the kitchen, and then he heard her lift the lid to the ceramic jar. "Do you make him sit first?"

"Yup. But he'll try to snatch it from your fingers at the last minute."

She emerged from the kitchen, treat in hand, Dax in tow. The afghan was still draped over her shoulders, but didn't cover her entire chest or any part of her legs. Her calves were nicely shaped as though she might be a runner; even her slim ankles and peach-tipped toes suited him. Hard to tell if this was his punishment or reward.

She stopped, one palm on her hip while she stared sternly at Dax. "Are you going to sit for me?"

He dropped his butt to the floor.

When she lowered her hand, Dax started to lunge, and she jerked back the treat. "No, you don't. You sit pretty, mister."

Noah should've known better than to think she'd be a push-over. The whiskey had mellowed her, but the effect had to be wearing off. She seemed more like the woman who'd first walked into his office. Minus a whole bunch of clothes. And looking mighty damn fine.

His body tightened, and he shifted, hoping his jeans wouldn't get snug on him again. This made no stinking sense. He didn't lose control this way around women, hadn't since he'd been a teenager, and least of all with a potential suspect. The only thing he could figure was that deep down he was relieved she wasn't like the rest of the ladies who'd been staying at the Sundance.

There was no sport in them throwing themselves at him. Even Trace, the youngest of the McAllister brothers, who'd always been a bit of a hound dog, seemed to be getting tired of all the fanfare. Rachel was the culprit, slanting her web-site to cater to single women.

His tail slowing down, Dax cast a woeful glance at Noah.

"Don't complain to me. Looks like you've met your match, buddy."

"Okay," Alana said when she had the mutt's attention again. "That's a good boy." She lowered the biscuit, and Dax filched it from her fingers before she could change her mind.

He settled on his belly in his favorite spot, the braided rug in front of the dormant fireplace, the Milk-Bone snug between his front paws.

With a fond smile, her hands stacked over her chest, Alana watched him as though he were a beloved nephew who could do no wrong. "He's part Lab, isn't he?"

"That and border collie, I think, but could be something else thrown in. I got him three years ago from a rancher north of town. He was only a puppy, maybe seven months old, when someone abandoned him. Poor mutt was only skin and bones."

She looked up, her lips parted, her expression aghast. "I wouldn't have imagined anyone abandoning animals out here."

"You kidding me? People can be idiots everywhere." He saw that he'd shocked her again. Probably his tone. He had a low tolerance for the poor treatment of animals. "The thing about rural communities is that folks tend to feel that animals have to be useful. Not everyone regards a dog or cat as a pet. They have to be able to herd cattle or be good mousers to earn their keep."

She seemed to mull over the information. "What's Dax's purpose?"

Noah should've expected that question. "To keep me company."

Alana's lips lifted in a slow smile that warmed her eyes. "I knew you were a softy."

In the nick of time, he stopped himself from uttering a cuss word. "Just what the sheriff of Salina County wants to be called—a softy."

Laughing, she sat down on the couch again. She'd forgotten to slip on the pajama pants, and he wasn't about to remind her.

"Did you grow up here?" She huddled under the afghan, drawing it tighter around her shoulders.

"Born and raised on a small ranch about ten miles east of here."

"Oh." She paused. "Is it still there?"

"Yep."

"Why are you living here in town?"

"Do you live with *your* parents?"

"Oh, God." She visibly shuddered. "The mere thought of living with my mother can make me break out in hives."

The cop in him snapped to attention. Making unguarded small talk could tell him a lot. "Where does she live?"

"Manhattan." Alana sighed. "About two miles from me, but we're both busy so I only see her a couple times a month, usually an hour or so for dinner."

"What about your father?"

She stared at Dax, who'd finished his bone and was licking crumbs from the rug. "I don't have one," she said in a flat, matter-of-fact tone.

For the life of him, Noah couldn't interpret her subtle mood shift. She didn't seem angry or sad, precisely, which to his mind ruled out divorce, death and abandonment. So what then? He was good at reading people, but not her, which rekindled his uneasiness, and he wanted to keep her talking. "I see my parents once a week, Sunday dinner, like clockwork," he offered, watching her closely. "More out of duty than anything else."

She transferred her attention to him, her brows arching in surprise. "You don't get along with them?"

"We get along okay." He shrugged. "We just don't have that much to talk about."

"Do you have siblings?"

"Two sisters. One moved to Boise with her family, the other to Billings. That's why I make sure I get out to the ranch and see the folks, check if they need help."

"I know Boise. Is Billings in Montana?"

He nodded, looking for any tells but finding none. If she was one of the con artists Sheriff Moran was looking for, she'd know where Billings was. A bigger city would be prime stomping grounds for a grifter. "What about you? Sisters? Brothers?"

"Just me—and of course, my mother." Pretty clear good ol' mom wasn't her favorite person.

"Ever been married?"

She seemed startled at first, and then amused. "I'm a slave to my work. I wouldn't even be taking a vacation except our offices are being moved so I was forced to leave. And look how well *that* turned out."

Right then and there Noah decided she wasn't Moran's suspect. No reason to try that hard at pretending she was a career woman from Manhattan. Hell, he wouldn't be surprised if she was a high-powered attorney like Kara. "What do you—"

"Have you ever—"

They both spoke at the same time. He gestured for her to continue, and she asked, "Have you ever been married?"

"Nope." He caught the hint of a smile lurking at the corners of her mouth. "What?"

"I don't know, I guessed you to be the marrying kind."

He momentarily considered the notion. "I suppose I am," he said, and snorted at the way her eyebrows shot up. "Why the surprise?"

"I'm not used to a man admitting it. In my crowd commitment is a four-letter word."

Watching Dax abandon his search for crumbs and go sniff the carpet near Alana's feet, Noah shrugged. He wouldn't mind having someone to come home to, share his day with, warm his bed, but he wasn't actively trying to make it happen, either.

"Do you, um…" She paused, glancing away long enough to draw his attention back to her face. Her tongue had slipped out to moisten her lips. She quickly pressed them together as she met his gaze. "Have someone in mind?"

Coming from another woman, he'd know what she was

thinking, but Alana? Tough call. Before he could answer, her eyes widened, then she let out a yelp and shot up off the couch. And he about jumped out of his skin.

6

"ALANA." NOAH WAS ON HIS feet, glancing toward the window, then probing her face. "What's wrong?"

The afghan slid off her shoulders onto the floor, scaring Dax. The dog darted toward the kitchen, barking his head off.

"Oh, God." She felt like a fool with Noah standing there, an apprehensive look on his face. Laughter spilled out of her, nervous laughter that made everything worse. Especially when she tried to stop and ended up sounding as if she was in pain.

Noah took her arm. "Alana, calm down," he said firmly, his grip tightening. He was on full alert, the consummate lawman, his vigilant gaze tracking Dax and then again scanning the darkness beyond the window. "Did you see something out there?"

"No." She bit her lower lip. "God, this is so incredibly embarrassing. It was Dax...." She took a shuddery breath. "I'm really ticklish, and he licked the...bottom of my foot." She didn't want to tell him that Dax's cold nose had gone between her knees. Although she wasn't sure why that felt like an embarrassing admission.

Noah studied her face, his gaze narrowing as if he couldn't decide if he believed her. He moved to the window, peering out into the darkness. The curtains were only partially open and he pulled them closed. "You're sure someone isn't following you?"

"Me? Who would be following me?"

"I thought maybe you saw someone outside." He signaled to the dog, who came to sit beside him.

"I wish I could say I did. My reaction would've seemed far more dignified." Her hand was at her throat and she lowered it, slowly releasing a strangled breath.

Noah's gaze drifted down for a moment, then jerked back up to her face.

She knew her nipples were hard and obvious through the thin T-shirt. To suddenly cover herself would make matters more awkward. "I'm sorry I scared you."

His tense mouth softened into a faint smile. "I don't scare that easily."

She scooped the afghan off the carpet, then glared at Dax. "No licking...I mean it. Or no more treats."

That got his ears up and his tail doing a hopeful wag.

"I have to remember not to say that word," she added.

Noah briefly met her eyes, guilt flickering in the blue-green depths as if he'd been caught raiding the cookie jar. Or staring at her nipples. He switched his attention to Dax. "You got that, boy?"

Alana had already noticed Noah checking out her breasts again, and her bare legs. She didn't mind. In fact, his interest was not only flattering, but starting to raise her temperature. "It's getting late."

He consulted his watch. "Yeah, almost nine. Don't want the roosters getting a jump on us."

"Funny." She pushed her hair back. "It's eleven my time."

"I thought you city women would just be getting revved about now."

"Not this one. I hit the office early." Alana plucked at a

loose thread from the afghan draped over her arm, wondering what it would be like to kiss him.

He seemed sort of interested in her. Or was he just being friendly? Hell, he was probably just being a guy. Of course he'd *look*. She didn't want to risk getting tossed out on her ass. Or worse, being shown back to the jail cell. No, he wasn't the type to do that.

She drew a deep breath. "Honestly, I don't want to be in the way. If you have a book I could borrow, I can go curl up in my room and leave you to your routine."

"You aren't in the way, but I have plenty of fiction and nonfiction if you want to read." He pushed the drapes aside for another quick look before moving toward the recliner.

"Good, I'll need something to take to bed with me." She bit back a smile when he momentarily froze, obviously taking her words the wrong way. "Guess I'd better change."

"I'll go make sure Dax has enough water in his bowl."

She started to go left, and he went right. The living room was small enough that they did a little dance, trying to avoid a collision. Finally, he caught her shoulders and held her still.

"I'm confident we can figure this out," he said, the humor in his eyes getting to her on a primal level.

She'd thought intense and sexy was a good look for him, and humor was a staple on her wish list, but holy crap... She had to take a moment and regain her composure. She normally wasn't like this. Even if a man did spark her interest, it was rarely just because of his looks. Even if he did have a sense of humor, her list was a long one, and she knew beyond a shadow of a doubt that the sheriff of Tiny Town, Montana, couldn't fill half of her requirements.

Which might just be the point. She was staying with him for only one night. Even if she didn't get her things back, she could call her bank tomorrow, make arrangements with the woman at the Sundance.

Besides, Noah Calder was far too observant to miss the cues that she was attracted to him. Just because she hadn't acted like a twit didn't mean she was immune. If she was as smart as she thought she was, she'd give it a shot. Take a step closer, see if he responded. If he politely pushed her away, or pretended he didn't know what she was up to, she'd go hide out in the room until tomorrow.

"Noah?" She clenched and unclenched her fists. For God's sake, she couldn't even decide if she should touch him. Who was this person wearing his T-shirt? She was never indecisive or timid.

When he didn't respond, she forced herself to look into his eyes. Damn the man. She didn't know a single person who could remain so unreadable.

His hold on her shoulders loosened.

"I just wanted to thank you again," she said, refusing to break eye contact. She could play that game pretty well, too. Let him try to figure out what she was thinking. Wouldn't happen.

"Is that all?" His hands moved down her arms slowly, almost like a caress, then rested right above her elbows.

That was playing dirty. Was he daring her? She wanted to blink, wanted to swallow. She did neither. "No, it isn't." She stepped closer and laid a palm on his hard-muscled chest.

His only reaction was to grip her arms infinitesimally tighter. Other than that he could have been a statue, his face chiseled from stone. Not even an eyelash flickered, and his lips stayed in a stubborn straight line.

They stared at each other for what seemed like an eternity, and then he released her. Her disappointment had to show, no matter how hard she tried to remain stoic. Then she saw it in his eyes, fleeting as it was—he was disappointed, too. So what the hell?

"I'm sorry," he said, his voice a low, intimate murmur. Moving back, he gestured toward the hall. "Please, go ahead."

It hit her like a double shot of espresso. Now she understood. Someone like Noah wouldn't abuse his authority or her unfortunate circumstance by coming on to her. She had no such restrictions.

"I'm not done with you," she said, and reclaimed the distance he'd put between them.

She slid her arms around his neck, then hesitated a second to give him an out. When heat darkened his eyes, she did something she'd never done with a man. She pushed herself up on tiptoes.

He lowered his head and their lips touched, his firm and unyielding at first. And then he slanted his mouth over hers and slowly, expertly kissed her. She felt his hands come up to bracket her waist, felt her aroused nipples grow even harder against the soft cotton T-shirt. His skin was warm, almost hot at the back of his neck, and his rigid body started to relax, until the only thing stiff about him hid behind the fly of his jeans.

He smoothed his hands down to her hips, and she suddenly became aware that, stretched up like this as she was, the bottom half of her butt was exposed. She wore panties—really, really skimpy panties—which he'd soon discover if he lowered his hand just another few inches. Though right now she was far more interested in his increasingly demanding kiss.

He used his tongue first, stroking it across the seam of her lips until she opened for him. The room seemed to spin around her. His tongue delved and swept, and she savored the sweet yet spicy taste of him, the stubble of his jaw and chin grazing her skin. It dawned on her that she'd never before been kissed by a man who wasn't clean-shaven, and she not only liked the sensation but wondered how it would feel on her breasts.

Beside them Dax whined.

Alana gladly ignored him, but she could feel a shift in Noah. Unwilling for the kiss to end, she clutched his muscled shoulders and let him taste her eagerness. Pulling her closer, he thrust his tongue deeper in her mouth.

Dax, the little bastard, pressed against her leg and whined again.

That did it. The kiss fizzled, and Noah slowly lifted his head.

Alana quietly groaned, dangerously close to throwing a mini tantrum. Except she was far too breathless to expend that kind of energy.

Instead, she pinned the mutt with an accusing glare. "I used to think you were cute."

Noah touched her cheek, and she realized she'd focused on the dog so she wouldn't have to look the man in the eyes. Her gaze went to his damp mouth, which did nothing to slow her pounding heart.

"I hadn't planned on that," he said, his fingers lowering from her face and trailing past her collarbone and between her breasts.

She shivered, then at his prompt withdrawal, whimpered in protest.

He cleared his throat, let his gaze pan the front of her shirt as he moved back, forcibly shoving his hands into his jeans' pockets.

"I started it," she said, when she saw a shadow of regret in his eyes. "I wanted you to kiss me." She caught his arm. "I wanted to kiss you."

"I don't need your gratitude. I'm just doing my job."

Alana laughed without humor. "I know how to say a simple thank-you. That had nothing to do with gratitude."

Almost as though he couldn't help himself, he slid his gaze to her chest. He was still hard, and she wished she had the nerve to pull her shirt off, tempt him into breaking down. In different circumstances, she would've been okay with that tactic. But she was out of her element and uncomfortable being at someone else's mercy, someone she couldn't quite gauge. She liked knowing her opponent before taking action.

His forearm was rock hard beneath her palm, and when she knew there was no budging him, she moved in closer. She traced a small circle on his skin, then followed the ridge of muscle up toward his elbow, and bumped his hip with hers.

She heard his sharp inhalation, and was pleased when he pulled his hand from his pocket. Alana pressed her palm against his and then brought his hand down to the hem of her shirt. It wasn't necessary to show him what she wanted; he reached underneath and covered her bare breast with his large, callused palm.

Her eyes drifted closed, every part of her springing to life, aching for his touch.

"This isn't right," he murmured hoarsely. "Jesus." His lips brushed hers and his fingers toyed with her nipple.

Gasping, she pressed against him, empowered by his re-kindled arousal. She managed to unfasten two buttons of his uniform shirt, enough so that she could slip her hand inside and feel the smooth warm skin over lean muscle.

He muttered a mild oath. "This is wrong." He jerked when she dragged the back of her other hand across his fly. "You're in my custody."

"Custody?" she echoed with a laugh. "Are we role playing?"

His entire body tensed, and she knew even before he removed his hand from under her shirt that her hope of a forbidden night with a stranger had just crashed and burned.

"I'm only teasing," she said, lightly stroking his belly.

He manacled her wrist and firmly pulled her hand away.

"I'm an ass," he said. "An apology isn't good enough, but it's all I've got."

"Noah, no…"

He moved far enough away that it was clear there would be no repeat of the last few minutes. Then he totally ignored her while checking the front door lock and pulling the curtains tighter.

She bent to pick up the afghan, and when she straightened, he and Dax were already headed toward the kitchen. A few seconds later she heard the back door slam.

Alana didn't understand his stupid code, not even a little, because it wasn't as though he was responsible for her in any way. The hell with him. Let him go freeze his buns outside and smooch his dog if that's what he wanted. Because she sure as hell wasn't about to beg.

NOAH FILLED HIS MUG WITH coffee, then leaned against the kitchen counter and listened. It was early in the morning but he knew she was awake. She'd left the bathroom a few minutes ago and returned to her room. The 1920s house was too small for much privacy.

He still couldn't get over the fact that he'd kissed her last night, had been willing to go further. Served him right that he hadn't fallen asleep until after two-thirty. Instead, he'd lain awake, waffling between wanting to pull that goddam T-shirt off her, and disgusted with himself for getting physical in the first place.

Man, she had nice breasts. Perfect legs. She was whip smart, too, and had a sense of humor. All ingredients that made for a good scam artist…or a New York exec. He still didn't know what she did in the city, or claimed to do. His subtle questioning had gotten sidetracked. Maybe by design on her part. Who the hell knew at this point?

After he'd convinced himself that she was innocent, simply a victim of circumstance and coincidence, she'd poked a hole in his confidence. Alana had claimed Dax had tickled her, and God knew the dog had a penchant for licking, but Noah could swear her reaction came after she'd been peering at the window. It wouldn't be a stretch to consider her partner might've followed her.

On the other hand, Noah's gut was telling him that she wasn't the grifter. Which meant that someone in his town had stolen her belongings.

Dax finished the last of his kibble, trotted to the door, sat and stared at Noah to let him out.

"I don't know, boy." Sighing, Noah opened the door. "Hate to admit that at my age I'm still thinking with my dick."

The mutt apparently didn't have an opinion. He darted outside, hot on the trail of a fleeting red-tailed-hawk shadow.

While sipping his hot black coffee, Noah watched the dog through the screen for a minute, then turned to find Alana entering the kitchen.

"Good morning." Her hair was still tousled, and she had a sleepy look in her brown eyes. Her smile seemed strained. "The coffee smells good. Hope you plan on offering me some."

"Help yourself." He indicated the blue mug he'd left on the counter for her. "There's milk in the fridge. Sorry, no cream."

"Thanks." She still had on his black T-shirt, but he couldn't help noticing she wore a bra. The plaid lounge pants were baggy and rolled up a few times, one leg an inch higher than the other.

He waited until she fixed her coffee, then asked, "You sleep okay?"

"No." She took a tentative sip and wrinkled her nose. Not surprising, since he tended to make the Colombian blend strong enough to strip the paint off his truck. She set the mug down on the Formica countertop and stared at it. "I'm sorry about last night." She finally looked at him, her expression chastened. "I'm not used to drinking on an empty stomach...." She huffed out a breath and returned her gaze to the mug. "No, I can't blame the whiskey. I wanted to kiss you and I went for it. That's it, that's the truth. I apologize if I made you uncomfortable."

Noah smiled. The only thing uncomfortable had been the fit of his Levi's. "Yeah, it was a real hardship."

She slowly turned her head, her eyes narrowed on him. "You aren't upset?"

"Only with myself."

She studied him for a second, the tension around her mouth easing. "Care to explain?"

"I'm not a kid. I know better than to act on impulse."

"So...it has nothing to do with you being the sheriff."

"Hell, yeah, it does."

"See, I don't get that."

Well, now she was just being ornery. He set his mug on the counter. "I gotta go fill Dax's water bowl."

"You can at least answer me first."

"Didn't hear a question," he said, and let the screen door slam behind him. Seconds later he heard it open. *Ah, Jesus.* She couldn't take the hint and stay put.

"Noah, wait."

"I like you better sheepish," he muttered, bending over to scoop up the bowl.

"I was just going to ask what time the bank opened," she said sweetly, and gave him an innocent smile that didn't fool him for a minute.

He glanced at his watch. "Not for a couple hours. We have time for breakfast, then for me to check in at the office. Ah, hell."

"What?"

"It's Saturday. The bank's closed."

She moved back from the door to let him in. "I thought all banks were open half a day on Saturday."

"Ours isn't." How could he have forgotten what day it was? Because she was distracting him, that's how, and no good was gonna come out of that scenario.

Noah headed for the landline, since he'd left his cell in the charger in his bedroom. Herman Perkins was the bank manager and he would open for an emergency. As long as Noah caught him before the old guy left to go fishing.

When Noah couldn't get an answer, he tried Pauline, the only other person who worked at the bank. But she didn't have a key and wasn't willing to do anything without Herman's permission, anyway.

Alana waited for him to hang up, leaned a hip against the kitchen counter and looked at him over the rim of her mug. "What's going on?"

"What happens if you call your bank directly? You know anyone working there well enough?"

She took a thoughtful sip, then pursed her lips, which he hated to admit distracted the hell out of him. "I have a contact who handles my investments, but he wouldn't be in today, and I don't know his number in the Hamptons."

"Last night you mentioned your mother...."

Alana stiffened. "Nope. Not an option. I'd rather sleep on that cot in your jail until Monday." She sighed. "Please don't make me do that."

He smiled to himself and walked over to the coffeepot to refill his mug. "You can stay here for the weekend."

"I'll have to borrow some money, or maybe you can vouch for me at the store and I can run a tab."

"What? You don't like my clothes," he said, eyeing the black T-shirt and wishing she'd skipped the bra.

"Only if you plan on keeping me locked up here."

"The thought crossed my mind."

"Why, Sheriff…" She cocked her head to the side, eyes sparkling, those lush lips lifted in amusement. "This is getting more and more interesting."

He was an ass. Teasing her like this was only going to get him in trouble. What he should do was turn her over to Roy for watching. At least then Noah wouldn't be tempted to cross the line that existed between a sheriff and a victim… or a criminal. Problem was, all he really wanted to do was kiss her again.

7

SHOPPING IN ABE'S VARIETY WAS certainly entertaining. The store was half the size of Noah's two-bedroom house and crammed with everything from athlete's-foot powder to peppermint chewing gum.

Alana dropped a hairbrush into her shopping basket, then stopped at the rack of costume jewelry and picked up a pair of silver hoop earrings the size of bracelets. Who wore these?

"What you've got there is genuine silver plate," Abe said, studying her over the reading glasses that rested high on his ruddy, bulbous nose. "It's the last pair in the store."

"Very nice," Alana said, and returned them to the rack. She wished Noah hadn't implied that she could shop till she dropped and that Abe shouldn't worry about the bottom line.

Well, Noah hadn't phrased it quite that way, and she wasn't concerned about how much she spent, but the owner was virtually drooling as he hovered, thinking he was in for a big sale. Something that most certainly wouldn't happen. Not here, she thought, as she regarded the array of dated merchandise, the meager sampling of T-shirts, underwear and socks packaged in threes.

Okay, so anything she bought would be worn only for a few days. Just until her luggage was recovered. And if it wasn't? The idea depressed her. It wasn't the clothes; they could be replaced. But her passport and her absolute favorite pair of earrings had been in the inside pocket of her purse. In fact, the handmade brown leather satchel was also a favorite, something that she'd picked up in Florence three years ago.

She held up a pair of Levi's. They were horribly cut, much more suited for a man. Loath to ask him anything, Alana glanced over her shoulder at the owner. "Are these the only jeans you have?"

His gray brows shot up toward his receding hairline. "What else is there besides Levi's?"

"Right," she murmured. "Thank you."

A woman's rusty chuckle came from behind the rack shared by magazines and every flavor of beef jerky known to man. At least Alana assumed it was a woman, one who apparently hadn't kicked her cigarette habit.

"You're only gonna get the basics here." A slightly heavy-set, fiftysomething brunette grabbed a *Country Living* magazine and limped toward Alana. "You want something pretty you best try Virginia's. Or even Louise's Fabric Shop. She has some ready-made sundresses, though it's a bit chilly for dresses. I'm Sadie. I own the Watering Hole down the block."

"What are you doing, sticking your nose around here and hijacking my customers?" Abe said, but he didn't look upset. If anything, he had a sparkle in his faded blue eyes that hadn't been there a minute ago.

"Be quiet, old man. Can't you tell this is a lady of quality? Think she wants to wear these?" Sadie held up a package of pastel-colored panties. The first pair, a pale pink, read Sunday in fancy black script.

A short laugh escaped Alana. This had to be some kind of joke. There was a hidden camera somewhere.

Sadie tossed the package back onto the heap between the white T-shirts and men's briefs. "Noah asked me to check up on you, see if you need anything. Damn shame your things being stolen in the middle of town right under everyone's nose. Never heard anything like that around here."

"I'm still hoping it was a kid's prank and that everything will turn up intact." Alana paused, looking for reassurance.

The woman offered none. "The news has got people scratching their heads. Most folks don't even bother locking their doors. Bet they all did last night."

Alana's optimism slipped a few notches, and she decided she'd better take this shopping expedition more seriously. "You said something about a Virginia's?"

"Yep." Sadie eyed Alana's navy blue slacks, the same ones she'd worn yesterday, along with the Armani blazer she'd pulled over Noah's T-shirt. "On second thought, I doubt Ginny's got anything in stock to your liking."

The woman's assessment wasn't critical or judgmental, but that didn't stop Alana from feeling defensive. "I don't need anything fancy. Lady's-cut jeans would be nice, and anything other than a T-shirt."

"I'll take you over there." Sadie picked up a package of white cotton granny panties, squinted at the size marked in the corner, then tossed it into Alana's basket. "Sorry, but Abe's your man for panties," she said, louder than necessary.

"Yep, Sadie, you're a real hoot and a holler," Abe called out, shaking his head in disgust.

The woman's mouth spread in a self-satisfied grin. "Any other toiletries you need, you best get them here. A few years ago we were all set to get one of those real nice Family Dollar stores built south of town so we wouldn't have to drive to Kalispell for everything Abe doesn't carry. Then the economy went kaput…." She shrugged. "Now that the Sundance is open and doing well maybe we'll see some life breathed back into this poor town."

Not if their guests kept getting robbed on Main Street, Alana thought. "How far is Kalispell from here?"

"Forty, forty-five minutes, depending on who's behind the wheel." Sadie sorted through bundles of socks. "I'd drive you myself except I got nobody to tend bar this afternoon. You pick up any brassieres yet?"

Alana hadn't heard that term before, though she knew what Sadie meant even without looking at the package the older woman held up. "Don't tell me—white, industrial strength only."

Sadie's gravelly chuckle turned into an awful wheezing cough. She turned her head and covered her mouth, muttering an apology.

"You okay, Sadie?" Abe asked, concern creasing his face and bringing him out from behind the counter.

"I'm fine." She waved him off. "It's my bronchitis acting up."

"I see your leg ain't healed yet, either. You been to see Doc Heaton?"

She waited until the coughing fit subsided and nodded. "I saw him." She shook her head with self-directed disgust. "Sorry about that. Didn't mean to blow out your eardrums."

Alana awkwardly patted the woman's arm. She wasn't good at this sort of thing, but Sadie was obviously mortified. "Your leg—I saw you limping. I assumed it was something more permanent."

"Nah, I got a good-size gash near my ankle from a broken bar glass. Last year I found out I got the sugar diabetes. Doc says sometimes it slows down the healing process."

"Oh, for pity's sake," Abe muttered. "How many times do I have to tell you that there ain't any other kind? Just say diabetes."

Sadie glared at him. "It's a wonder you have any customers, you ignorant old goat."

Hiding a smile, Alana concentrated on sifting through the meager selection of bras, though she'd pretty much decided that she'd end up washing hers out each night. She was picky about lingerie.

"Bet Doc also told you to stay off your feet," Abe continued. "Instead of steering my customers to another store, you should be taking it easy." He pretended annoyance as he straightened items on a shelf, but his concern for Sadie was clear. "Hope you aren't planning on tending bar and waiting tables all afternoon and tonight, too."

"Gretchen is coming in at six," Sadie said with a sigh. "Couldn't get her or Sheila to come in sooner." It was as if a switch had been flipped and she remembered who she was talking to, because she suddenly frowned at him. "Not that it's any of your business."

"Dang stubborn woman," he muttered as he returned to the register.

"You know what?" Alana returned the granny panties to the shelf. She didn't want Sadie walking her anywhere. If necessary, Alana would find Virginia's on her own later. "I think I prefer these, after all." She scooped up the day-of-the-week bikini panties. "With my day-planner stolen, at least with these I'll know what day it is."

Sadie started to laugh again, but caught herself before she aggravated the congestion in her chest.

Alana turned to give the woman privacy, noticed a package of T-shirts in different colors and tossed it into her basket.

"Here's a slim cut that should fit you." Sadie held up a pair of Levi's against Alana's hip. "Good length. You shouldn't have to roll them."

"Perfect." She draped them over her arm and surveyed the contents of her basket, everything from deodorant to a charcoal eye pencil and mascara. "This should do it."

"I reckon Noah will have a sweatshirt he can loan you

when it gets too chilly in the evening," Sadie said, and Alana didn't miss the sly glance that passed between the two busy-bodies.

"Did you want to know if I'm staying with him?" Alana asked, directly meeting each pair of blue eyes. "If so, I'd suggest you ask the sheriff."

"Hell, we all know you're staying at his place. Can't keep a thing like that secret in Blackfoot Falls. What we don't know is which room you're staying in, his or the guest room."

"Oh, God. You people need more entertainment in this town." Alana moved to the register and set the basket on the counter. She kind of liked Sadie, but wasn't about to get that chummy with her.

"That's a fact," the woman said. "The boys are getting tired of shooting pool and feeding the jukebox. At least since those gals from the Sundance have been popping in, the younger hands don't go spend their paychecks in Kalispell every Friday and Saturday."

"You have a real jukebox?"

"The genuine article."

"You know, I've never seen one."

"Tell you what. After slowpoke here finishes ringing you up—" Sadie looked pleased when she got a snarl out of Abe "—we'll go by Virginia's and Louise's. Then I'll take you to the Watering Hole. I don't open for another hour, but I gotta set up, and you can play some tunes on the old girl. I'll even spring for the quarters."

"I'd like that, but no more shopping for me. I'll get my luggage back soon." When Abe rang up the final item, out of habit Alana reached for her purse, then sighed.

"What does Noah say?" Abe was bagging her purchases, but he stopped what he was doing. "Is he of the mind your things will suddenly turn up?"

Sadie set her magazine on the counter, her brows knitted

in a frown as she waited intently for Alana's answer. In fact, both she and Abe looked as if there was nothing more important at this particular moment than what their sheriff had to say. Clearly, they put a lot of stock in Noah's judgment.

"I don't know," Alana said slowly. "He's a difficult man to read."

Grinning, Sadie dug into her jeans' pocket and laid out some bills. "Not to folks who know him. He's as uncomplicated as a man could be. Though I'm still not sure why he came back. But we're lucky to have him."

"Came back?" Now who was being nosy? Alana couldn't help it; if she had the chance to learn something about the man, she wasn't about to lose the opportunity.

"After his stint in the army and then college, he went to Chicago." Abe passed her the bags and glanced at Sadie. "What was it, three or four years?"

"There about. He was a policeman. Said he liked it." Sadie picked up her magazine, leaving the bills on the counter. "You can keep the two cents," she told Abe, then turned to Alana. "You ready?"

Alana had more questions, but she heard the bell over the door, signaling a new arrival. Not anxious to make any more friends, she hurried along. "Abe, do you have a receipt for me, or something I should give Noah?"

"I'll take care of it," he said, waving her off and greeting his next customer.

On their way to the bar it troubled Alana that Sadie's limp seemed to have gotten worse. None of her business, she reminded herself. As the woman put her key in the door, Alana looked up at the sign for the Watering Hole and flashed on the horrific moment yesterday when she'd realized everything had been stolen.

The space between the buildings really was more of a walkway than an alley, though someone could easily have wheeled her suitcase to a waiting car in the back lot. It would've had to have been spontaneous. Unless someone had seen her coming from the edge of town and waited right here while an accomplice distracted her. Highly unlikely. This wasn't New York.

"There was a time when I wouldn't even bother locking this place," Sadie said, turning the key, then using her shoulder to bump the door open. "Over the years I've had the odd bottle of whiskey or vodka go missing, but nothing to lose sleep over. And I'm not talking about the recent thefts. I started locking up when the—"

"Recent thefts? This has happened before?"

The abrupt interruption had Sadie visibly recoiling, and Alana could see that look in her eyes, knowing she'd said the wrong thing, but unsure how to rebound.

Alana wasn't about to let this slide. If he'd lied to her... "Noah said that what happened to me was an anomaly."

"A what?" Sadie's puzzled frown seemed genuine.

"Unusual," she said, brimming with impatience. "That thefts were out of the ordinary in Blackfoot Falls."

"That's true enough." She seemed to relax. "It's outside of town where there's been some trouble the last two months." She flipped on switches that produced the typical murky bar lighting. "Things have gone missing from the surrounding ranches, sometimes small items, sometimes equipment. Noah is still hunting down the McAllisters' horse trailer that was taken in August." She tossed her magazine onto the bar, then pulled out one of the chairs at a table and sat down. "You ask me, it's been too long and they're never gonna find that trailer, which is a damn shame because that's something those poor folks don't need to lose." Sadie gestured vaguely. "Put your bags down and take a load off."

Alana took a seat across from Sadie, who'd pulled up her pant leg and was probing the area around a large white bandage. "Has it gotten worse?" Alana asked, noticing the red puffy skin.

"About the same." She tugged her jeans down. "Noah didn't lie to you. Everyone thinks the ranch thefts have to do with transients. In the past, the ranchers always had enough work to go around. This year they've been turning down men right and left. That don't mean those men still don't have mouths to feed."

Alana breathed in deeply and glanced about at the dozen tables and mismatched chairs. In the far back were a pair of pool tables. The place was bigger than it looked from outside, but it was quite drab. "You said your business has improved since the Sundance opened?"

"Better, but still so-so. Now if some of the other ranchers who are struggling decide to start taking in tourists, I expect I'd be able to breathe easier. Might have to fix up the place, though," she said with a rueful smile. "Make it more female friendly, if you know what I mean. That is, if I can come up with the money."

"It shouldn't cost too much," Alana said, noticing the quaint mirror behind the bar that had a very Old West feel. "I could kick around some ideas with you, if you want. It's what I do back in New York. I'm in advertising."

"I knew you were one of those smart career women." Sadie grinned. "I could tell right off." She pushed herself to her feet. "You're on vacation and I don't wanna ruin that, but if you got any ideas, I'd be eager to listen. In the meantime, best I get busy. That jukebox we were talking about is in back. I'll scrape up some quarters from the till."

Alana had totally forgotten about the jukebox. Although she wouldn't mind having a look at it, she didn't like the idea of Sadie being on that bad leg. "What is it you have to do in order to open?"

The older woman stopped at the massive mahogany bar

and rested against it. "Wipe off tables that I should've taken care of last night, make sure I have enough clean glasses, cut up limes, that sort of thing. Why?"

She shrugged. "I figured I could help."

Sadie regarded her with an element of shock. "Well, now, that I didn't expect."

"Me, neither," Alana said with a smile. Normally she was allergic to manual labor. That's why she had a housekeeper come in twice a week. "Noah is working, and frankly, I don't have anything else to do." Okay, so she also hoped to find out more about the sheriff. But no one had to know that.

"You're gonna get your nice clothes dirty," Sadie said, eyeing the navy blue slacks and high heels.

"No, I won't." Alana picked up the bag with her new Levi's and T-shirts. "You have a place where I can change?"

Sadie stared at her for a long, silent moment, with keen eyes that seemed to see too much. "Head on back past the pool tables. You'll see the ladies' room door on the left."

Without another word, Alana did just that, hoping like hell she wouldn't regret the gesture. But then, really, what was the worst that could happen?

8

IT WAS EARLY AFTERNOON BEFORE Noah returned to his office feeling as if he hadn't had a chance to breathe since breakfast. Half a dozen calls had him and Roy hopping from one ranch to the next. Roy should've had the day off after working last night, especially since he was on for Sunday. But Noah only had two other deputies—Danny, who was sick with the flu, and Gus, who worked part-time and was away for a few days.

Typically, that would've been just fine. But with everyone jumpy because of the latest theft, normally rational folks were ready to pull the trigger if they saw a mouse dart across the barn floor. What a mess.

As soon as the office door closed behind him, Noah yanked off his hat, tossed it on his desk and plowed his hands through his hair. After threatening to string up half the population of Salina County for being dimwits, he hoped the rest of the weekend was more peaceful. Of course, he still had Alana to deal with.

He took a look at his watch and cursed. He'd asked Sadie to check up on her, but that had been almost three hours ago. There weren't enough stores in Blackfoot Falls to keep Alana busy for that long. With all the thinking he'd done about her, the images that had intruded at the most inconvenient times, how had he let so much time go by?

He scooped up his hat, set it back on his head and left the office without checking for messages. Though most everyone knew his cell number and didn't hesitate to keep him on speed dial, even if it was only to rescue a cat that had climbed too high.

On his way out the door, he tried calling his house, hoping she was there. No answer. He glanced down Main Street, shaking his head at all the tacky Halloween decorations. The Blackfoot Falls Betterment Committee, or so Louise, Mildred, Sylvia and the Lemon sisters called themselves, had gone all-out. They were even urging people from Cutter's Crossing and Maryville to come to the festivities planned for next Friday night. Just what he needed. More strangers and mischievous kids traipsing around town while he tried to get a handle on the thefts.

He didn't bother checking Abe's place. No way would Alana still be there, shooting the breeze with the usual Saturday crowd that drifted to the variety store after eating at the diner. They'd all be busting with curiosity and peppering her with questions. He had a hunch that wouldn't turn out well...for anybody.

The Watering Hole had already opened for business, and he figured Sadie would be his best bet to locate Alana. He just prayed she hadn't skipped town. No, dammit, she wasn't Moran's suspect. Noah had already decided she was innocent. She'd spooked him for a minute last night, but he knew Dax had a bad habit of licking.

It took a few seconds for his eyes to adjust from the bright sunlight to the cool dimness of the bar. No sign of Alana. He hadn't really expected to see her in a place like this, yet a part of him hoped he'd find her here and the damn tightening in his chest would ease.

Sadie stood behind the bar, streaming beer from the tap into a pitcher. A husky young man Noah didn't recognize, and who barely looked old enough to shave much less drink, sat across from her, a half-filled mug and a stack of quarters in front of him. In the back, a pair of Circle K hands glanced up from their game of pool and nodded to Noah. One of them was Sam Miller. Noah had run into the guy because a couple of pissed-off fathers had pulled shotguns on him. Seemed Sam had a way with the young ladies.

"Afternoon, Sheriff." Sadie set the pitcher on a tray, then wiped her hands on the towel draped over her shoulder. "You still on duty, or can I get you a beer on the house?"

"Still on the clock." He adjusted his hat and eyed her young customer, who gave Noah a nod before lowering his gaze to his badge.

"Don't you worry. I checked this fella's ID." Sadie chuckled. "He made it just under the wire."

Something about the kid struck him wrong. "You working at one of the ranches?" Noah asked him, keeping his tone casual, though nowadays a new face tended to make him edgy.

"Yep. I started at the Gunderson place last month." He shrugged a beefy shoulder, staring down into his glass. "Wasn't until last week that I could legally come in here."

"Getting old ain't all it's cracked up to be, Tony," Sadie said to him, then winked at Noah. "You looking for someone in particular?" she asked slyly.

"You know where she is?"

Tony used the back of his sleeve to wipe his mouth as he glanced toward the rear of the bar and the pool tables. The smile that crept onto his face wasn't one Noah would like to see in a back alley fight.

He looked around the room, but didn't see Alana, and relaxed.

Sadie's grin was a whole other story. "She's been helping out until Gretchen gets here."

Noah frowned. "Alana?"

"Did someone call for me?" She came around the corner from the direction of the bathrooms, stopping abruptly when she saw Noah. She smoothed her hair with the back of her wrist, straightened her shoulders and then continued to walk toward him. "I hope you're here to save me."

She wore a red T-shirt with the sleeves pushed up to her elbows, the hem tucked into Levi's that were rolled up above her ankles, and she was still wearing those high heels. Her hair was pulled into a messy ponytail, though half the shiny brown strands hung loose, either curling around her face or clinging to her flushed cheeks.

Noah stared, not generally prone to speechlessness, but what the hell? He felt as if he'd landed in one of those parallel universes in a Syfy channel movie. The only coherent thought he could muster was that she'd look just like that right after sex.

It took him a moment to work up enough saliva to swallow, to remind himself that he was the damn sheriff. "Save you from what?"

She stopped on the other side of Tony and cocked her head at Sadie. "For your information, I will never do that again. Ever. But it's done." She frowned at the mug of beer sitting in front of Sadie. "That better not be yours, and you know why."

Sadie shoved the ale toward Alana. "Don't get your panties in a wad. It's for you. Figured you'd be thirsty by now."

Only when Alana peeled back a yellow rubber glove to check her watch did Noah even notice she was wearing gloves. "It's barely afternoon."

"Ah, hell, live it up. You're on vacation."

Alana let out an unladylike snort, then covered her mouth. "Yeah, right, some vacation." She pulled off the gloves, rolled them up and ducked behind the bar as if she owned the place. She put them somewhere, then went to the sink, washed her hands and knew exactly where to find a towel. With arched brows, she eyed Noah. "Where have you been?"

Even though he was looking at Alana, he could feel Sadie's gaze burn a hole in the side of his face. She was likely waiting for his reaction to Alana's bossy tone. "Working."

"Finding my purse and luggage?"

"Not yet."

Her wince told him more than words could have. He didn't blame her for being upset. Most people these days had their lives on their phones. A smartphone was like a personal assistant who held the keys to all the locks. But then she pursed her lush pink lips, which got an entirely different kind of reaction from him.

Letting out a heartfelt sigh, she slid her hand into the front pocket of her Levi's. "Here," she said, holding out two twenty-dollar bills. "Abe didn't give me a total, but when you settle up with him you can put this toward my purchases."

Noah stared at the money. "Where did you get that?"

Sadie and Tony both chuckled.

Alana glanced toward the back room. "I won it off Sam and Hector."

"Shooting pool?"

She shrugged. "I warned them I was good."

"That she did," Sadie agreed, animation taking ten years off her weary face. "Beat 'em in record time, too."

"Jesus, Sadie, how long you gonna rub our noses in it?" Sam hollered from the back.

"Till I get good and tired," she called in answer, and set two frosty mugs with the pitcher of beer before picking up the tray.

Alana stopped her. "Why are you standing? It's not necessary." She pointed to a chair set behind the bar. "I'll take this," she said, and waited for Sadie to do as she was told before picking up the tray with both hands, not looking too steady as she carried it toward the back room.

She had a nice sway to her hips, something Noah had noticed yesterday. Tony was showing his own obvious appreciation as he stared at her backside. Even though it was hard not to watch Alana walk all the way to the tables, Noah found himself wondering about this new kid. It was odd, now that he thought about it, that Gunderson had hired a hand when winter was coming on. As far as Noah knew, the ranch owner hadn't fired anyone lately. On the other hand, the old buzzard was looking pretty haggard—probably more to do with drinking than working hard.

Still, Noah would check with Cole and Jesse, see if they'd heard anything about this kid. He seemed earnest enough, but something was itching the back of Noah's mind, and he'd learned from long years with the military police and the force in Chicago to listen to that itch.

From her perch, Sadie planted her fists on the bar and leaned forward until she could see the pool tables. "You can tell she never had to waitress a day in her life." She laughed quietly. "That one was born giving orders."

Odd that Sadie didn't seem to mind. In fact, she sounded like a proud mama. Of course, she more often than not resembled a drill sergeant herself.

"The beer is on me, gentlemen," Alana was saying at the back, lifting the pitcher and mugs off the tray and setting them on a table. "It was a pleasure doing business with you."

"Come on…." Sam took his shot, missed the pocket, cursed as he straightened. Casually pushing back his long blond hair, he used his cue stick to block her path. "You're not leaving."

"I am." With one finger she lifted the stick and moved it out of her way.

He flashed her a cocky smile. "You gotta give us a chance to win back our money."

Alana laughed. "You can't beat me. I'll just take more of your paycheck."

Sam's hopeful expression dimmed. "Hell, you're probably right." He cast a swift glance at Hector, who was smiling and shaking his head, letting him know he was on his own. "Let's play for a buck," Sam called after Alana when she started toward the bar.

"Another time, maybe."

"Come on, sweetheart," he drawled in that brash way of his. "You sure I can't change your mind?"

Her steps slowed. Judging by the piqued glint in her eyes, she didn't like being called sweetheart. "Pretty sure," she said drily.

Oblivious to her sarcastic tone, Sam angled his head to the side and watched her walk the rest of the way toward Noah and Sadie.

"I should take his last dime," Alana murmured, and pulled another two twenties out of her pocket. "How much for the pitcher?"

Sadie's grin was a mile wide. "You keep it, *sweetheart*."

At Alana's openmouthed indignation, Noah smiled.

"You're just a riot, Sadie." She laid both bills on the bar. "Hope this covers it."

"They might get away with charging that much for a pitcher in New York. If I did that, I'd be out of business."

Alana left one twenty and pocketed the other. "Guess I should keep some just-in-case money on me."

"I wish you'd take this other one, too," Sadie said. "After all the work you did around here, I should be paying you."

"You mean that?" The slightest of smiles lifted the corners of Alana's lips.

"I said it, didn't I?"

"Then keep your butt planted in that chair as much as possible and that'll be my payment." She touched Tony's arm. "Are you going to be here awhile?"

He nodded.

"Remind her to take it easy, will you?"

"I'll do just that." He leaned back to look at her, and dammit but there was something about the kid that bugged Noah.

"Thank you." With a strained smile, she moved her hand. "So, Sadie, when did you say Gretchen will be here?"

"A couple of hours. Won't start getting busy until after four."

Alana absently nodded, as if she had a hundred things swirling around in that head of hers, and then she looked at Noah. He was beginning to think she'd forgotten he was there. "I have to get my bags from behind the bar, but I'm ready."

"Sure thing, your highness." He checked his watch for emphasis, not because he was on a schedule. "Take all the time you want."

Raising her brows, she moved her shoulder in a flippant shrug. "Fine. If I'm bothering you, I'll stay here with Sadie."

"Get your bags."

She stared at him for a long, charged moment, the desire to tell him to go to hell plain in her eyes. Instead, she let out a long-suffering sigh. "I guess it doesn't do to argue with the town sheriff."

He should tell her to stay. He had a mountain of paperwork to do, and she'd likely be bored. But he didn't want her shooting pool with Sam Miller or getting chummy with any of the other hands. Mostly because he didn't completely trust her yet, but part of his reluctance was plain personal.

While he watched her sashay around the corner of the bar, from his peripheral vision he caught Sadie studying him. He slid her a sidelong look, and she gave him a small, shrewd smile. God only knew what was going through *her* head.

But as far as gossips went, Sadie was on the lower end of the scale, and in here, with people liquored up half the time, she heard it all.

She switched her attention to Alana. "You gonna drink your beer, or should I give it to Tony?"

"I'll pass, thanks."

Noah relieved her of the two bags. "How about some lunch?"

"We just had breakfast."

"Over five hours ago."

Her brow wrinkled. "Marge's?" she said, with the enthusiasm of a hen entering a fox's den.

He didn't have to look around to confirm that everyone had their antennas up. And they sure didn't need to know he planned on taking her home and making sandwiches. "We'll see."

"Come back anytime," Sadie called out as Noah opened the door. "We'll make small talk. I swear on my mama's grave, no cleaning involved."

Alana shuddered. "Stay off that leg."

"And I thought I was a pushy broad." Sadie's laugh turned into a wheezing cough that followed them out to the sidewalk.

Alana hesitated, glancing back at the door. "Does she have family here?"

"Not anymore. She and her husband divorced years ago, and her daughter lives somewhere in Oregon." They started walking again, but he could tell Alana's mind was far away. "Why?"

"She's not that well and she doesn't take care of herself." Alana tugged down the sleeves of her T-shirt. "It's getting chilly."

"What do you mean, she's not well? Other than that cough."

"She has diabetes and a gash on her leg that's healing too

slowly. And yes, I'm fully aware that it's none of my business."

Noah liked Sadie, always had. She had a gruff manner but a big heart. "Has she been to the clinic?"

"She said she saw Dr. Heaton," Alana said. "I helped her change the bandage and got a good look at that cut. Frankly, it's hard to believe it's already two weeks old."

"Heaton's a good doctor." At his street, Noah touched the small of her back to steer her into a right turn. "Somehow I didn't picture you as a bandage-changing kind of gal."

"Normally, I'm not. But things have been pretty damn weird since I arrived in your little town." Her eyes lit with surprise and she gave him an unexpectedly sweet smile that made him wish he'd touched her for a different reason. "Oh, we're going to your house."

"I put a few groceries in the fridge earlier."

"You went shopping?"

"I was out at the Rocking P ranch, and Libby Perkins gave me fresh butter and a loaf of bread she'd just pulled out of the oven. So I stopped at the Food Mart for some deli meat."

"She made bread?"

Noah smiled. "Most people do around here."

"I didn't think I was hungry, but I've changed my mind."

"Yeah. The smell was killing me all the way back to town." With a brief nod, he acknowledged Gloria Sealy, who lived two doors down from him and was busy sweeping her pristine front porch. Even from fifty feet away he could feel her curiosity coming in waves. He'd bet that in two minutes she'd be on the phone to Marge, asking about Alana. "What was that back there about you cleaning?"

"Oh…that." She sighed. "It needed to be done. Besides, I had no idea what I was really getting into or I would have run the other way. I definitely have to give my housekeeper a raise. Cleaning is— What's that look for?"

"Nothing." Would the woman ever cease to bewilder him? "Nice of you to pitch in."

"I'm going to have nightmares for weeks."

He grinned. "Couldn't have been that bad." They got to his gate and he opened it for her.

"We'll see when I wake you up at midnight." She was trying to keep a straight face, but her lips quirked.

If this were a minute later, after they'd closed the door behind them, he would've kissed her. He might've given himself a swift kick afterward, but the desire to feel those soft lips was too powerful to deny.

She stared into his face, the pulse at her throat beating wildly, as if she could read his every thought. "Then maybe you shouldn't sleep alone," he said, and her eyes widened. "Dax can keep you company."

"You bastard." She laughed and shoved his arm. "Ooh, nice." She fondled his biceps, molding her palm over the bunched muscle. "You must work out."

"Uh, I think my neighbor's watching."

"Exactly." Her mouth curved in a triumphant smile.

"Okay," he said, with a drawl that promised retribution. "I'll remember this."

"Bring it on." She walked ahead of him, exaggerating the sway of her hips, then waiting at the door.

He laughed to himself. They'd probably just made Gloria's week. By the time she got on the horn and finished re-creating what she'd witnessed, she'd have him engaged to Alana.

"Go ahead," he said. "I left it unlocked."

Once they were both inside, Alana went for the bags, but he held them out of her reach.

She stared at him, first in surprise and then with a mischievous gleam in her eyes. "Sorry, but I didn't pick up anything in your size."

"No more fooling around in front of the neighbors."

"And when we don't have an audience?" she asked in a low, sultry voice, her chin lifting in challenge.

He fantasized for a moment about how she'd react if he stripped off her shirt and Levi's, and showed her exactly what he wanted to do. "Here." He pushed the bags at her.

Startled, she hugged them to her chest and regarded him with a disappointed gaze. "Are you ever just Noah and not Sheriff Calder?"

Damn good question. The best thing about living in Chicago had been the anonymity and having time to himself. But he'd known what to expect by coming back to Montana. The trade-off was being here for his parents. His sisters had done their part while he'd gone off to college and sampled city life. It was his turn.

"I'll be in the kitchen," he said, removing his hat. "Hope you like ham."

"Hey, maybe later we can use your handcuffs."

He shook his head, tried to block the image of her cuffed to his four-poster bed. "I ought to arrest you for gambling."

She grinned. "I have a feeling you'd have to lock up half the population of Blackfoot Falls."

More like the entire county. "Mustard or mayo?"

She let out a frustrated sigh. "Buzzkill."

"Mustard it is."

"I'll make my own sandwich," she said irritably.

He smiled then, as he watched her kick off her heels, scoop them up and pad down the hall to her room, barely resembling the woman who'd walked into his office only yesterday. Problem was, damned if he wanted it to be Dax who shared her bed tonight.

9

IT WAS EARLY, THE SKY STILL dark outside in the dawn hour
before the sun rose over Blackfoot Falls. Dead tired, Noah
rubbed the rough stubble along his jaw. If he had a brain that
was in working order he'd be crawling into bed instead of
sitting in the kitchen drinking coffee on a Sunday morning,
after working most of the night. He was taking the day off
no matter what. God help anyone who tried to haul him out
for a nuisance call.

"You're home."

He looked up at Alana standing in the doorway, her hair
tousled, her eyes sleepy. He hadn't even heard her stir.

She wore a T-shirt similar to the black one he'd loaned
her, except this one was cream-colored, made it only to the
tops of her bare thighs, and it was real clear that she wasn't
wearing a bra.

His cock twitched. So maybe he wasn't as tired as he
thought.

"Mornin'," he said, when he figured he'd stared long
enough. "Hope I didn't wake you."

The sleeves were too long and reached her knuckles. "No,
I thought I smelled coffee, but I assumed you had it on a

timer." She bent over and tugged up the white socks sagging around her ankles.

Her T-shirt slid up, and he couldn't help but notice her panties were high-cut and pink.

"I eased up on the amount of coffee. It's not as strong today."

"Your house, your coffee. Make it as strong as you want."

"You're welcome."

She smiled and grabbed the mug he'd left out for her. "I hope you didn't just get home."

"About half an hour ago."

"You've been working straight through since nine-thirty?"

"Yep."

Her coffee poured, she sat across from him, her leg bumping his under the table. "Sorry." She angled away. "Does that happen very often, getting called out at night?"

"Not really."

"I didn't think anyone was awake that late around here." She took a sip. "There can't be much to do other than going to the Watering Hole...." She abruptly lowered her mug, her eyes alarmed. "Was there trouble there?"

"Not that I heard about. If the boys get a little rowdy, Sadie can handle it."

Watching Alana gaze toward the window and push her fingers through her tangled hair, he understood now why he hadn't gone straight to bed. Fool that he was, he'd wanted to see her when she woke up, when she was still fuzzy-headed and relaxed. Although she wasn't quite as uptight as he'd first thought. For a woman who'd lost all her things, she was rolling with the punches pretty smoothly.

What the hell was wrong with him? He knew better than to cross professional lines. Yet he sure hadn't done a good job of hiding his attraction to her, and damned if she wasn't doing her best to tempt him.

He told himself he wouldn't do it, wouldn't look there, and then immediately lowered his gaze to her chest. Her nipples pressed against the cotton, which was thin enough that he could see they were a dusky color. She bumped his leg again, and he snapped out of his daydream of pulling up that shirt and having a taste.

"Want more coffee?" she asked, pushing back from the table.

Man, he couldn't get up, not in his condition. "Thanks," he said, and passed her his mug.

"Can you tell me what the emergency was?"

"What emergency?" He twisted around and watched her lean a hip against the counter as she picked up the carafe.

"Last night."

"Oh, that… No big deal."

"No big deal," she echoed, turning to stare at him, confusion in her eyes and maybe even a little hurt. "You were gone eight hours."

Ah, now he understood. She thought he'd stayed away on purpose. "We had a couple of saddles go missing, but I expect they're gonna turn up."

"Another theft?"

"Maybe. Probably not. There's some history behind the saddles, and I'm pretty sure they were borrowed without permission."

Alana nodded, but he wasn't sure she believed him. He wasn't sure he'd told her the whole truth.

"Then we got a call about a missing husband. He told his wife he was rounding up strays, and when he didn't come home after dark and wasn't answering his cell, she called and asked if I'd go check on him. Turns out he'd gone to Kalispell with a couple of buddies, got drunk and passed out."

Alana blinked. "What an ass. His poor wife—she had to be worried sick."

"Worried, and madder than a wet hen when she found out where he'd been." Noah arched his back and stretched his arms over his head, stiff from spending so many hours in his truck looking for the stupid kid. "They're both young, married only a few months—mainly because Linda is pregnant, I suspect."

"Being young is no excuse for being that irresponsible and cruel," Alana said quietly, and went back to pouring their coffee.

"I agree. I wasn't excusing him." The story had obviously hit a nerve. "A lot can happen to someone riding an ATV alone after dark. I had no choice but to go look for him, so I'm not happy with Brett, either. Not to mention Linda was hysterical and bawling when I hadn't found him by early morning. She was really laying into him when I left their place an hour ago."

"So you haven't slept." Alana set his coffee in front of him, and startled him by putting a hand on his shoulder.

"Not yet."

"I hope you don't have to work today."

His heart slammed in his chest with her this close. He wanted to pull her onto his lap, bury his face between her breasts. Take her to bed with him. She removed the temptation by withdrawing her hand and reclaiming her chair.

He pretended to fight a yawn just in case his voice failed him. "Roy's on duty. He likes working Sundays so he doesn't have to go to his in-laws' for dinner."

She smiled. "Nice to know everyone is so happily married around here." Wrapping her hands around her mug, Alana gave him a long, measuring look. "You seem tired. You should take a nap."

"What are you gonna do?"

"I don't know. I read until after midnight. Maybe I'll get a couple hours more sleep myself."

There was a long, charged silence while they sat there staring at each other. Teasing aside, Noah had a feeling if he asked her to join him in his bed she'd readily agree. All the years he'd been sheriff, he'd never been in this position with a woman. Lines had always been drawn and clear. This situation with Alana was blurry as hell, although he couldn't say why, since technically she wasn't a suspect. He was just helping her out. So why hadn't he called Rachel and asked her to make room at the Sundance? He had no right to keep that option from Alana.

"I'm not used to coming home and having someone here," he said finally.

Her lips parted and she scrambled to her feet. "You were trying to unwind, and I just barged in on you."

"No, don't go." He'd really stepped in it. "I don't mind you being here." She seemed unconvinced and ready to leave. "It's kind of nice. Dax never asks me how my night was."

Her slight smile indicated she thought he was just being polite. "Where is he, anyway?"

"I let him out when I got home. Hasn't come back yet."

She walked toward the window and looked outside. The sun hadn't risen, so she couldn't see much. He had a feeling he'd made her uncomfortable, and he was sorry about that. But he didn't want her to go.

"When did you learn to play pool?"

"In college." She turned around in surprise. "Where did that come from?"

"I was going to ask you last night before I got called back to work."

"We had a table in the basement at my sorority house. A friend taught me to play, and I used it as a stress reliever." Alana's mouth twisted wryly. "Which meant I played almost every evening. Anyway, turned out I was really good, and I like winning."

He reared his head back. "I never would've guessed pool would be your thing."

She sniffed. "Nothing wrong with that. Do you play?"

He was waiting for that question. "I used to. Not much anymore."

"Are you any good?"

"Do you mean good enough to go up against you?" he asked, and saw the spark of challenge ignite in her eyes. "I don't know. I didn't see you play."

"Are you better than Sam and Hector?"

"Oh, yeah."

She came back to the table. This time when their legs touched, she didn't move hers. She leaned forward, the T-shirt stretching snugly across her breasts. "Play me."

"Where?"

She frowned. "The Watering Hole, I guess."

"No, the Sundance. The McAllisters have a pool table."

Alana leaned back and studied him for a moment, her eyes narrowing in suspicion. "Why there?"

"More privacy."

She laughed. "In case you get beaten by a girl?"

He shook his head, even though she was half-right. "I have to be careful. I don't like drinking in public and just hanging out, even when I'm off duty."

"I get it. You want to protect your image." She grinned. "And not let everyone see you get beaten by a girl."

"You're pretty damn cocky," he said, aware of his own competitive instincts rising to the surface. "Hey, keep it up. Be smug. It'll work in my favor."

"Think so?" She was really looking full of herself now. "We should play for something." Her nonchalant shrug didn't fool him. "A small friendly wager."

"Around here, when people get serious, they play for money or pink slips. You don't have either."

"Hmm. No, I don't...." She paused, working up to the kill and looking so cocksure it irritated him.

He motioned with his chin. "I'd settle for winning those pink panties off you."

She blinked and her mouth dropped open, the smugness wiped from her face. For a minute she seemed to struggle for words, and then a wicked smile slowly lifted her lips. "You want them that badly? I'll give them to you right now." She reached under the hem of her shirt, then shifted in her seat as if she was actually pulling them off.

Damn, he couldn't tell if she was bluffing. She *had* to be bluffing. Then again, she was constantly surprising him. Only one way to find out, and he'd always been good at playing chicken. He watched and waited.

While he willed his excited cock to friggin' settle down.

Their gazes met and held, and when it became obvious she was taking too long to be doing the deed, he did everything in his power to tamp down a smile. One hint that he was feeling victorious, and she'd show him.

Wait a minute...what the devil was wrong with him? Did he really want to win this round? Or did he want to force her hand?

Noah grinned for all he was worth.

She frowned slightly, her worried gaze slowly moving over his face. "You're playing me...." she murmured. "Aren't you?"

"Me?" he asked with his best poker face.

She bit her lower lip, then reached under the table. "Here you go." She threw the pink panties at him.

He caught them against his chest, the silky feel of them soft under his palm. Yet not an expensive texture he'd expected from her. He held them out, then laughed at the cursive "Sunday" across the back. "Abe's Variety?"

She exhaled sharply. "I give a man my panties...I don't expect him to laugh."

Noah balled the fabric in his hand. They were so skimpy they fit in his fist. "What *do* you expect?"

She actually blushed. "You practically dared me to take them off," she said, her voice a little shaky. "I don't like to be dared."

"Good to know." And man, did he mean that. He pushed himself back from the table and saw her swallow convulsively. Though he had her cornered, he wouldn't gloat. Not so much because he was trying to be a gentleman, but if he gave her reason to sharpen those claws, she'd recover too quickly. He liked seeing her off balance and uncertain.

She barely moved, just followed him with her eyes. "Are you going to lie down?"

"Not yet."

"You realize you have to be the one to leave the kitchen first," she said, tracking his path to the back door.

"Why?" He checked for Dax. No sign of him.

"You know why."

"Nope. Can't say that I do."

"Then give those back," she said, holding out her hand.

He came back, caught her wrist and pulled her to her feet, ignoring her startled yelp. "You want them?"

Without the high heels, she was a good eight inches shorter than him and had to tilt her head back to meet his eyes. She lifted her chin, drawing herself as tall as she could. "Besides pool, the other thing I did to relieve stress was kickboxing."

He pulled her closer. "Wearing no panties? That could be interesting."

She huffed out a laugh, her expression tinged with excitement. "This isn't very sheriffy of you."

"Where did you go to school?"

"Yale."

He should've known she was an Ivy Leaguer. "They teach you words like *sheriffy?*"

Alana bit her lip. "Come on, Noah, fair is fair." She suddenly sounded businesslike, even as she twisted her wrist free and slid her arms around him. "Boxers or briefs?" she asked, and ran her hands over his ass. "Or do I have to find out for myself?"

"I'm not telling."

Her lips parted and she stared into his eyes, issuing a silent challenge of her own.

He reached under her shirt and cupped her bare breasts, watching her eyes drift closed, her lips part a little wider. As hard as he tried to contain himself, he shuddered at the feel of her pearled nipples pressed to his palms, her fluttering heartbeat. Knowing that she had on nothing below drove him crazy. All he had to do was slide his hands lower....

His heart pounding, he brushed his mouth across hers, moving his head until he was at the perfect angle, and bit lightly at her quivering bottom lip. Her soft whimper went straight to his cock and pushed her taut breasts against his palms. Her fingers dug into his backside and she pulled him closer until his erection pulsed hot between them.

Reluctantly, he released a breast and skimmed his hand over her hip, around to the firm curve of her buttock. Giving the smooth flesh a light squeeze, he pushed his arousal against her tense, feverish body. What he wanted was to reach between them, find her wet and ready for him to bury himself inside her. The battle for control and patience strained him to the breaking point.

In the breathy quiet, the phone rang.

No, he had to be wrong. *Please, God, be wrong.*

The insistent ringing echoed off the muted-yellow walls— not his cell, but the landline—and Alana shrank from him. She tugged at the bottom of her shirt, her cheeks flushed and her gaze skittering.

Dammit, he wanted to ignore the intrusive sound, yank the

phone from the wall to make it stop. He looked at the clock over the door. No one called this early on a Sunday unless it was an emergency.

Shit.

He kissed her, fast and hard, and then drew in a deep breath before lunging for the receiver in the middle of the fourth ring.

"Sheriff Calder."

He heard the slurred murmur of his mother's voice and briefly closed his eyes. She'd already been drinking. Or more likely, she hadn't been to sleep yet.

"Mom, it's six-thirty in the morning."

He glanced at Alana and shrugged apologetically. She seemed to be in a daze. He knew the fog had barely lifted for him. But he hoped she'd leave in case the conversation got tricky. The kitchen phone had a cord, so he wasn't going anywhere, although he didn't plan on talking long.

"I didn't wake you, did I, son?"

"No, I was awake."

"I wanted to check with you about supper tonight."

"I talked to Pop yesterday and told him I wasn't coming." Noah rubbed at the suddenly tense spot at the back of his neck and carefully avoided Alana's gaze. "Didn't he tell you?"

"He did, but I don't understand. You never miss Sunday dinner. Did I do something wrong?"

"No, Mom, it's not you. You know better." He hated turning his back to Alana but didn't know another way to hint that he needed privacy. "It's work related."

"Everyone knows where to find you on a Sunday evening if they need you."

Luckily, she didn't sound as drunk as he'd initially feared. But she wasn't usually this adamant, either. "I'll come another night. Maybe Tuesday or Wednesday. How's that?"

"It's tradition, Noah. The family is supposed to sit down

together on the Sabbath." Her voice caught. "You know how hard it is for your father and me since your sisters left."

His father didn't give a damn about what happened in that house anymore, and Noah could hardly blame him. Though there was no point in taking that road. He loved his mom and at the same time hated that she drank herself into stupors.

He sighed and turned to glance at Alana. She was at the door. It was beginning to get light, and she'd apparently found something to stare at outside.

"Okay, Mom, maybe I can swing dinner tonight." He had to be getting punchy to even consider this, he thought, staring at Alana's back, at her long bare legs. "But I have a guest, and if she wants to come with me, I'm bringing her."

Alana heard him. He knew because she straightened with a slight jerk and then smoothed back her tangled hair. She didn't turn around, though.

"A woman?" His mother sounded excited. "I didn't know you were seeing anyone."

"I'm not. She's—a friend...from out of town. I'm sort of helping her out."

"Oh, yes, do bring her. I can bake a pie. What kind do you think she'd like?"

"That's not necessary." Already he regretted bringing up the idea. Most times he ended up making dinner. "Will you feel up to having company?" he asked calmly but pointedly.

After a brief silence, she said, "I'll be fine, Noah. I promise you."

He smiled sadly. He doubted she had a clue as to how many broken promises had strained the family ties. "Let's keep the meal simple, okay? I'll help when I get there."

"You're a good son. Have I told you that lately?" she asked softly.

"Why don't you go rest for now? I'm gonna do the same. I'll see you around five."

After he hung up, he waited until Alana turned to face him. Her arms started to lift to her chest, then detoured to tug down the hem of her T-shirt. She gave him a tentative smile.

"You don't have to come," he said, not bothering to pretend she hadn't overheard.

"I want to," she said without hesitation, surprising him, because he'd misread her body language.

But obviously, she had something else on her mind. He wasn't sure he wanted to hear it. Man, what a difference a lousy phone call could make. A few minutes ago he'd wanted to drag her into his room and lay her down on his big bed. And now... "Alana—"

"Shh." She moved closer and put a finger to his lips. "Talk later. Sleep now. Go."

When he tried to kiss her, she gave him a gentle shove toward the hall. Amazing. She knew exactly what he needed.

10

ALANA ROUTINELY PITCHED IDEAS to multimillion-dollar clients and sometimes spoke at seminars to audiences of a hundred or more people. Rarely had she been nervous, not even her first day on the job. But pulling up in front of the modest brick ranch house in Noah's truck had her clenching her hands.

"I can't believe I let you talk me into wearing this awful T-shirt and Levi's. And to Sunday dinner on top of everything. Your parents will think I'm a total slob." She eyed the old barn that was sorely in need of paint and repair, then looked at Noah. "What?"

"I'm wearing a flannel shirt and jeans," he said drily.

"That's different. You're their son."

"And you're their son's friend." He turned off the engine. "If you'd worn your fancy silk blouse and tailored slacks, my mom would be jumpy and wishing she'd dug out her mother's china."

Alana watched him lean back and sigh quietly. He didn't seem as rested as he should be after sleeping for seven hours. "What are you going to tell them about me?" she asked.

He shrugged. "The truth."

Which version? she wondered. For all she knew Noah made a habit of taking in strays. He seemed to be the type.

Maybe that's all this was between them; he was a rescuer and she'd needed rescuing. Oh, hell, what did she expect? It wasn't as if he was taking her home for dinner for any other reason than to be nice.

God. The altitude was making her soft in the head.

"They must be wondering why we're sitting out here so long."

"Nah, Dad's either in the barn or out in the pasture, and Mom's in the kitchen, which faces the mountains." Noah reached for Alana's hand, then gave her a smile that warmed his blue-green eyes. "I want to kiss you."

Her heart fluttered. "Where did that come from?"

The smile faded. "Today did not go as planned."

"Oh, you had a plan?"

"It was my day off. And I had a half-naked woman in my kitchen—"

"Shut up, dammit. You aren't allowed to bring that up."

He stared at her in amusement. "You're blushing."

"I am not." She was. Heat stung her cheeks for the second time in two days. What was with this crazy Montana climate?

Smiling again, Noah leaned over and kissed her briefly on the lips. She wanted more, much more, and just the thought of it made her flush again. If she could get away with it, she'd convince him to turn the truck around and go back to his house.

"You're evil," she said, her breathing a little ragged. This was so high school she couldn't stand it. "Now I have to go meet your parents."

She looked away, wanting to get her act together before she went inside. But one quick glance at the house had her turning back to Noah again, fast. "Oh, crap, your mother's at the door."

He smiled as if he didn't believe her, and started to lean toward her once more.

"She can see us. Please, Noah."

He frowned and glanced out her window. His mother waved. "Well, shit."

"Okay, I'm waiting in the truck."

"I have tinted windows. Don't worry about it." He opened his door. "Even if she saw us, she's not going to say anything. It was just one friendly kiss."

"That's not the point."

"Oh, great. Here comes my dad with his shotgun. He'll make you marry me for sure."

Alana practically shrieked, her gaze flying toward the barn.

Noah laughed. "I'm kidding." He got out, then came around the hood and opened her door. When she hesitated, he said, "I could bring your dinner out to the truck, but that might raise some awkward questions."

"Told you…you're evil." Alana let him give her a hand down. It was a really big truck, not at all like getting out of a Yellow Cab.

She smoothed her hideous red T-shirt and walked alongside Noah toward his waiting mother, who stood holding the door open. Alana was relieved to see the woman also wore jeans, paired with a blue sweater that matched her eyes.

"Hello, you two. Come on in," she said, all smiles. Her sandy-blond hair was pulled back into a neat ponytail. Her cheeks had a rosy glow and she had a reasonably trim body, but up close she looked older than Alana had expected.

Noah kissed his mother's cheek, then held the door open above her head. "Go on in, Mom. I'll make the introductions inside."

"Please, come in," she said to Alana, the excitement in her voice and eyes really quite sweet.

Alana followed her inside, Noah right behind.

"I'm Celia." She dragged her palm down the front of her

jeans, then appeared to be trying to decide between a hand-shake or a hug.

Alana settled it by extending her hand. She'd never been a hugger. "I'm Alana Richardson," she said. "So nice to meet you, Mrs. Calder."

"Oh." She waved off the formality. "Call me Celia. Son, don't wear your hat in the house."

"Right." With a faint smirk, he removed the Stetson, which left a slight ridge that had Alana wanting to push her fingers through his hair. He hung the hat from the top of an oak coat tree standing near a grandfather clock. "Where's Pop?"

"In the barn, as usual." Celia offered an apologetic smile. "I'm sure he heard your truck and will be along in a minute. Please, make yourself at home," she said to Alana, and gestured to a small, cozy room with a worn but neat plaid couch and two brown overstuffed chairs angled on either side of a brick fireplace. "What can I get you to drink? We have beer, coffee, wine, whiskey...."

"Wine?" Noah snorted.

Celia sniffed. "Yes, Chablis." She gave him a quick glare as if to tell him to quit being a heathen. "I keep a box of it in case we have guests."

Noah's mouth opened, and the second the teasing glint entered his eyes, Alana cut in.

"Chablis would be nice, thank you," she said quickly. "Would you like some help?"

"No, please sit." Celia wiped her hands on her jeans again. The poor woman seemed nervous, as though she didn't have many guests. "I'll be right back."

Alana noticed the knitting basket tucked beside one of the overstuffed chairs, and a pipe in an ashtray on the table next to the other. So she took the couch, then crooked her finger for Noah to join her.

While she carefully occupied the right side, Noah sat in the middle, close but not touching, which was surprising considering how he spread his legs in typical male fashion.

Still thinking about the wine, she leaned over and whispered, "I think your mother's very sweet. And she's clearly trying her best."

He cast her a swift, curious glance. "What do you mean?"

Alana blinked. "I didn't mean anything...." He'd told her nothing about his family other than his sisters had moved away with their families. "I got the impression your parents don't have company often."

"No, they don't," he agreed with a slight frown. "I'll likely have to help her with dinner." He paused, studying Alana for a moment. Probably waiting for her to offer her services, which she'd already done and was really glad about being turned down. "Okay?"

"I can set the table and pour beverages." She wasn't sure what she'd said to earn her a funny look, but she glanced in the direction she presumed was the kitchen and let out a frustrated sigh. "I can't cook."

He smiled. "We're not having anything fancy, I promise you that."

"No, I mean, I really can't cook. Boiling an egg, yes, I can manage, but that's about it."

Shrugging, he said, "Mom's not such an ace in that department, either. That's why I might have to help."

Pleased, Alana settled against the couch. "I like her more already."

He was sliding an arm along the back, leaning toward her, when a loud bang startled them both.

Instantly alert, he jumped to his feet. "Mom, you okay?"

"Fine," she called out. "I dropped a pan."

"Stay here." His face drawn in a concerned frown, he walked at a fast clip toward the rear of the house.

Alana's impulse was to follow him so she could help, but

she did as he asked, wondering what was nagging at her. Something wasn't right. Noah was a laid-back guy, but from the time they'd left his house she'd sensed an aura of tension around him. Nothing obvious, in fact so slight she could easily convince herself that it was her imagination.

After all, she barely knew the man, so it was pretty absurd that she was giving the matter any thought. He might simply be nervous about bringing a woman home, lest his parents get the wrong idea. God, just thinking about introducing a man to Eleanor was cause enough to hyperventilate.

They were taking a really long time, so Alana got up to look at a collage of pictures hanging on the hallway wall. She smiled when she saw the photos of a young Noah, clearly high-school age, one with him in a football jersey, another in a tux and boutonniere, looking stiff and ready to bolt. Even as a teen he'd been broad and muscular.

Several other photos were of two women who had to be his sisters, both of them blonde like their mother, and with stunning blue-green eyes similar to Noah's. And the kids…wow. A studio portrait of a gorgeous towheaded toddler with a round cherub face, long curls and big blue eyes was flanked by older twins with the same light hair, same eyes. All three kids could easily be used in print ads. They had to be his nieces. Alana wondered if the pursuit of modeling careers for the girls was the reason his sister had left Blackfoot Falls. Sad for Celia. She had to miss her grandkids like crazy.

Alana's mind drifted to Eleanor. So not the grandmotherly type. She'd probably check herself into a psych ward if Alana even got pregnant. Though she doubted that would ever be an issue. Alana couldn't see herself as a mother. Sometimes it bothered her that she didn't have a single maternal instinct. Her career was what motivated her.

At least she knew where she stood. Eleanor had had no business having a child.

"Sorry I took so long." Noah passed her the white wine, filled to the brim of a sherry glass. "It was this or a tumbler," he said, his gaze going to the collage. "Those are my nieces."

She noticed he didn't have a drink, and wondered if he might have to go to work later. "Is everything all right?"

"Yep." He peered closer at one photo of the twins. "Cute kids, huh?"

"They're beautiful. Truly. They could be models if your sister wanted. When did she move?"

"Vicky left six years ago, and it's been about three since Tina packed it in."

Odd way to put it, Alana thought, studying him for a moment before looking again at the pictures. "The kids weren't born here, then?"

He pressed his lips into a thin line. "No. They visit once or twice a year." His voice had lowered. "Do me a favor and don't bring them up in front of my mom."

"No, of course not. She has to miss them. Guess it's up to you to fill the void."

He snorted. "Not likely."

"What? No kids for you?" Alana had absolutely no stake in his answer, and still her pulse quickened in wait.

"Didn't say that."

Expecting him to elaborate, she took a sip. It was pretty awful stuff, but then she was a certified snob when it came to wine. "I don't get it," she said, when it finally appeared he had abandoned the subject. "Either you want kids or you don't."

From the amused lift of his brows, she assumed he thought she was being nosy. She preferred to think of it as mild curiosity.

"I wouldn't mind having a couple, but I'm not going to get married just to have kids." He cast a fond look at his nieces. "What about you?"

"Oh, God, not me, I'd be a terrible mother."

"Why would you say that?"

"I have no experience with children. I had a dreadful role model. I'm completely selfish when it comes to my career. I have never been nor have I ever wanted to be responsible for another human being. Frankly, the thought terrifies me." She met his eyes, annoyed that she was feeling defensive. There was no reason for it. She was simply being honest, not trying to be popular or politically correct. "Does that answer your question?"

If he'd seemed repulsed or disappointed or shocked, none of those reactions would've surprised her. His sudden laughter caught her off guard. "Yeah, I think you've tied everything up in a nice neat package."

She frowned. "I'm not sure what you mean by that."

"I just heard the back door…must be my dad. Come meet him, and then you can watch me make the mashed potatoes and gravy. You might learn something," he said with a teasing wink.

Her eye roll spoke for her. She took another small sip of wine and followed him into the brightly lit kitchen with ruffled, pink gingham curtains and buttery-yellow walls. Celia was at the stove, and a tall, lean man with short dark hair stood at the sink washing his hands. His jeans and green flannel shirt were both faded, but his work boots were remarkably clean.

"Hey, Pop, I want you to meet Alana."

In no apparent hurry, his father shut off the faucet, shook the water from his hands, then turned as he grabbed a striped hand towel off the counter. He wasn't being standoffish, she quickly realized. It was just his laid-back way, much like his son's.

Giving her a friendly smile that reached his blue eyes, he made sure his hands were completely dry before he extended one to her. "I'm David Calder," he said. "Glad you could make it to supper with us."

"Thanks for having me."

He had a firm grip that made his welcome genuine and stirred something in her that was a bit unsettling. Due to her own bias, she'd expected someone different. She knew he was a rancher who'd lived his entire life right here, and she'd seen the rustic pipe near the ashtray, all of which, for her, hadn't added up to this handsome, distinguished-looking man. Put him in a suit, give him a decent haircut and he would've fit right in with the retired attorneys or judges who served on so many charity boards.

His palm was rough, though, and his skin tanned and slightly weathered. But for a man who had to be in his early sixties, he still had a relatively unlined face, and looked quite a bit younger than his wife. If Alana were Celia, she'd really hate that.

"Do I have time for a quick shower before we eat?" David asked Noah, and not his wife, which Alana found odd.

"Go ahead, Pop, I still have a few things to do."

"I have to put the biscuits in the oven yet," Celia said, as if to herself, and pressed her hands to her flushed cheeks.

The two men exchanged a cryptic glance, and then David left the kitchen and Noah went to work getting out bowls and whisks and other gadgets.

Alana set her glass out of the way. "Give me something to do."

"No, you're our guest." Celia spun around, her elbow catching a glass pitcher and knocking it off the counter.

Noah's hands shot out, his reflexes lightning fast, and he caught it not two feet from the floor.

Celia pressed a hand to her heart. "Thank you, son. You know that belonged to your great-grandmother."

He nodded, his mouth curving in a faint smile of someone who'd heard those words a hundred times.

The rest of the dinner preparation went by smoothly, with Noah doing most of the work. By the time they sat down to the meal of delicious-smelling chicken with all the trimmings, Alana couldn't decide which she was more starved for, the food or answers to the questions formed while observing mother and son.

Their complex and delicate relationship intrigued the hell out of her. Throw reserved, emotionally detached David into the mix, and if Eleanor had been here, she would've had a field day analyzing everyone.

"So you're from New York, is it?" Celia asked pleasantly, her food barely touched, her slightly unsteady hand reaching for the glass of wine to the right of her plate.

She was the only one who'd joined Alana in imbibing with dinner. Noah had had half a beer while making the gravy and whipping the potatoes. David quietly sipped black coffee while he ate. Alana had tried to stop her sherry glass from being topped off, but Celia had insisted.

"Yes, Manhattan," Alana replied, avoiding Noah's gaze, because this was the third time she'd responded to the inquiry since they'd sat down forty minutes ago. "The meal was incredible. I never have home cooking, and I've eaten so much I'm ready to burst."

"Is that your subtle way of trying to get out of doing dishes?" Noah had finished his second helping and started stacking plates.

"Alana is our guest," Celia said in a disapproving voice. She didn't seem as sharp as when they'd first arrived, and Alana fleetingly wondered if illness, medication or alcohol was the cause. "Besides, we still have pie."

Noah hesitated, and then with a small smile, patted his flat belly. "I don't think so, Mom."

Sitting at the head of the table, David was quiet, as he'd been through most of dinner, but he looked like a man who really wanted a smoke. Or to be anywhere else.

Celia ignored her husband and son. "Alana, how about a piece of apple pie? It's my specialty. The trick is extra cinnamon," she said, the last few words coming out painfully garbled.

Though no one said anything, Alana felt the tension coming at her in waves. Noah sent her a quick glance that indicated it was time to go, then picked up the stack of dishes. David watched Celia reach for her wine, the resignation in his eyes unmistakable as he pushed back from the table and murmured an excuse to slip away.

Celia sighed, her shoulders sagging in helpless defeat.

Alana toyed with her napkin. So this wasn't the Norman Rockwell picture she'd expected. At least Celia was trying, and Alana couldn't let the evening end on this note. It would be horrible…for Celia, for Noah, for everyone.

"Alana, how about some help with washing the dishes?" Noah stood in the doorway between the kitchen and dining room, his expression pointed.

"Sure," she said, purposefully keeping her gaze even with his. "Right after I have some of your mother's pie."

11

HIS SHOULDERS AND NECK TIGHT from tension, Noah brought the pie to the table, along with dessert plates and a carafe of fresh coffee. He didn't know what the hell Alana was up to. No way she hadn't figured out his mother had had too much to drink. Why stay and prolong the agony? He'd made it pretty damn plain that it was time to leave. Jesus, they'd made it through dinner without an incident. He didn't want to press his luck. The pie? Who knew how that had turned out. Though Celia had kept herself together up until supper.

He'd made peace with his mother's drinking problem years ago, and he'd even forgiven… No, not forgiven. He now understood why his father had emotionally distanced himself from her. It had nothing to do with not caring, or giving up. That was the only way a person could live with a drunk on a daily basis. His dad still loved her, just as Noah did. Detaching from the behavior meant you could stay and not go crazy or end up hating. The emotional separation allowed you to be real clear that there wasn't a damn thing you could do about it except be there if and when the time came that she decided she'd had enough and wanted help. He'd read enough books, talked to enough recovering alcoholics, to know he was doing the right thing.

The "if" part was still hard, though. Sometimes Noah wanted to shake her, force her to face the fact that she was missing out on her grandchildren's lives. At one time she'd lived for the day she'd have grandbabies, and now they'd been taken from her because watching and waiting for the other shoe to drop was too painful for everyone. Had he been in his kid sister's place, he'd have done the same thing. The children had to be the first priority.

Although he knew Alana was watching him, Noah refused to look at her. He wasn't embarrassed by his mother; her problem was her shame to carry, not his. But he was a little pissed off at Alana for ignoring his cue to leave, and now wasn't the time to let it show.

Surveying the pie, knife, plates and clean forks, he asked, "Did I forget anything?" They were gonna eat their pie, fast, and then they would leave.

"The silver pie server would be nice. It'll keep the pieces intact," his mother said, sounding surprisingly sober.

He glanced at her, and she gave him a tentative smile, full of apology and pleading and gratitude all mashed up together. "Sure," he said, noticing that she'd pushed her wine aside and reached for the coffee carafe. "I'll get it."

Emotion welled in his chest. For one tiny second she looked like the old Celia, the mom who'd cheered louder than anyone at his varsity football games. Maybe he was too old to want that mother back, but he did.

He found the serving gadget sitting on the counter, and returned to the dining room. This time he did look at Alana while she was busy swapping stories with his mom. She seemed totally relaxed, listening intently, as if his mother were the most important person in Blackfoot Falls. When had someone last treated Celia Calder like that?

They both laughed suddenly. He didn't hear what was said,

but the sound snapped him out of his preoccupation. "Go ahead and cut the pie. I'll go find Dad."

"You know he's probably having his smoke." She shrugged at Alana and picked up the knife, a slight tremor in her hand.

"Would you like me to cut that?" Alana offered. "I can't have Noah accuse me of slacking off."

"Thank you."

"I'll try not to lick my fingers," Alana said, grinning, and his mother smiled back, any momentary awkwardness erased.

He found his father on the porch. Prepared to bodily drag him inside if need be, Noah was still relieved when it turned out that wasn't necessary. They all sat at the table again, each with a piece of pie.

"You said earlier your mother is a psychiatrist?"

At his father's voice, Noah jerked a look at him. He hadn't uttered more than a dozen words since they'd started supper.

Alana had just taken a bite of pie and nodded, touching a napkin to the corner of her mouth.

"You haven't mentioned your father."

She put her fork down. "I don't know him," she said with slow deliberation. "He's never been in my life."

"Oh."

Noah had to control a smile at the oh-shit look on his father's face. Poor guy finally opened his mouth and he ended up sticking his foot in it. Not really, but Noah knew that's what was going through his head.

"Were your parents divorced?" Noah asked, to get his father off the hook, and because Alana had evaded the subject yesterday.

"Never married." She picked up her fork again and focused on slicing off a bite of pie. "Eleanor used a sperm donor."

Of all the things she could've said, he wasn't expecting that explanation.

"You call your mother by her first name?" his mom asked, mild disapproval in her voice.

"She prefers that I do." Alana shrugged. "She isn't what one would call a conventional maternal figure."

Even in his mother's slightly inebriated condition, Noah doubted she missed the underlying sarcasm in Alana's tone. But the tinge of sadness in her eyes was what got to him. Though she tried to sound matter-of-fact, her eyes told the truth. She knew disappointment well.

"I was basically raised by a nanny until I went to boarding school. When I came home for weekends and holidays, the housekeeper was there when Eleanor wasn't. Grade school was a bit difficult. Even the kids with divorced parents had someone show up for functions. Sometimes I did wish..." She stared down at her pie and slowly carved out another bite. "This is delicious. I'd ask for the recipe except I wouldn't know what to do with it."

Noah smiled. His parents just stared at her.

Finally, his mother asked, "Does...Eleanor...live in New York, too?"

"Not far from me. We see each other a couple times a month, usually for lunch or dinner at a restaurant. I like keeping our visits to a time limit."

His parents shared a glance. They hadn't done that in front of him in a while. Then Celia asked, "Do you ever wonder about your—the man who fathered you?"

"I don't think of him as my father. He donated his sperm for money, which, by the way, I don't begrudge him. He didn't want to be a parent. Some people shouldn't be." Alana's lips curved in a sad smile. "Like Eleanor. Oh, I do love her and I'm grateful for the advantages she gave me. We simply don't—" Alana blushed, her eyes widening for a moment. "I'm sorry, I seem to have told you more than you needed to hear."

"Nonsense." Celia reached across the table and gave her

hand a hearty pat. "You've been the highlight of my week. It's nice to have someone to talk to. You're welcome here anytime."

Noah shoveled in his last two bites and chewed quickly. He wiped his mouth, threw his napkin onto his plate. "It has been nice, Mom, but we do have to go. I have to stop by the office and check in with Roy before it gets too late."

"Oh." She seemed disappointed, but then smiled. "When do you leave, Alana? Maybe you two can come back for dinner again before you go."

No guarantees were made, only that Noah promised he'd call later in the week. They said their goodbyes quickly, with hugs all around, after his father shocked him by offering to help wash the dishes so that they could start back to town. And it wasn't because he was trying to get rid of them. The man even stepped out onto the porch to wave. Another shocker.

It was a dark, moonless night, with nothing but trees and nocturnal creatures between the family ranch and Blackfoot Falls. Noah and Alana had driven for five minutes before she broke the silence. "You're mad at me for prolonging dinner, but I'm not sorry that I did," she said, keeping her gaze on the road ahead. "So if you're waiting for an apology you might as well give up."

"I don't expect one. No reason for it."

She turned to look at him. "They're nice people. I wish I could've met your sisters."

"And my nieces?" he asked, smiling.

"No, they would've scared me to death."

"Yeah, me, too, sometimes." He shook his head. "I don't envy my sister and brother-in-law when the girls get to be teenagers."

"Teenagers? Ha. Twelve-year-old girls are sexting boys these days."

Noah groaned. "Yeah, thanks for that."

"It's the truth. No sense sugarcoating things."

He let her words float around in his head for a minute, dissecting them three ways to Wednesday. "You think I should've warned you about my mother."

"Only if you think I should've kept my mouth shut about Eleanor."

He'd guessed at her intention during dessert, and her quick, impassive response confirmed his suspicion. Whether she'd admit it or not, she'd learned a few tricks from her mother. "I knew what you were doing and I appreciate it."

"What was I doing?"

"Deflecting for Mom, sympathizing, laying yourself open and making sure we knew you didn't come from a perfect cookie-cutter background." He smiled at her slack-jawed stare. "Do I need to go on?"

Finally, she sighed, a quiet sound of resignation. "You give me too much credit." She slumped back. "I got a little carried away with the sperm donor thing. Way too much information."

Chuckling, Noah shook his head. "You East Coast people…"

"What?"

"You call that getting carried away? Spend another afternoon at the diner or the Watering Hole."

"What does it have to do with being from the East Coast?"

"I don't know. I shouldn't have said that."

"People gossip and blab no matter where they're from. I hear it in the break room at work. I can't even grab a cup of coffee in peace. It drives me crazy." She reached over and rubbed his thigh. "You didn't, though. I respect that."

"Tell you about my mom?" It was hard to keep his focus with Alana's hand on his leg. He shrugged. "Not my story to tell. If I could take the burden from her, I would. But I can't.

I love her, and that's all I can do. Though I'm glad you didn't feel ambushed."

After a moment's silence, Alana said, "You're a great son, you know that?" She squeezed his thigh. Nothing sexual, more a friendly gesture, but his brain was having trouble communicating that to his cock. "And she was absolutely lovely. She's lonely and misses her daughters and grandkids."

"I know."

"But I understand." Alana cleared her throat. "I really do. Family stuff can be so damn complicated. See, if it had been my mother I wouldn't have been able to bear listening to her patronizing tone, seeing the bored look on her face. Only I would know, because she's excellent at hiding her feelings, but it would kill me. So in that regard, I apologize for drawing out the evening if it made you uncomfortable."

"You're pretty good at hiding, yourself."

"I am." She moved her hand. "I'm damn good at it. All those why-don't-you-have-a-dad questions when you're little really tend to toughen one up."

He hadn't meant to upset her. "When I was a kid, I hated to be in public with her, or around her at all. That's why I mostly hung out at the McAllisters."

"Is that why you moved to Chicago?" Alana asked.

"Who told you I lived there?" Noah wasn't necessarily surprised, more curious about what she'd heard. "Sadie?"

"Yes, she mentioned it. So did your mom. She said you came back after your older sister took off." Alana paused. "Your mom told me about the miscarriages, too."

"Did she?" Now that did throw him off. He'd hoped his mother didn't think about that dark time in her life anymore. But wasn't that part of the reason she drank? Naive and foolish of him to think she'd shaken off the past.

"Yes, she said that your sisters were ten and fourteen, you

were almost thirteen, and her getting pregnant had been a shock to her and your father."

Noah was glad when Alana stopped talking. God knew he was well acquainted with the rest of the story: the resigned joy, the miscarriage, the second miscarriage, his mom's descent into the bottle.

"I'm sorry. I don't know why I brought it up." Alana turned her head to look out at the darkness. "That's not true," she said, bringing her gaze back to him. "I was feeling defensive because I assumed you thought, ironically, that I'd been gossiping. So I very clumsily tried to let you know I came by the information honestly."

Noah smiled and reached over to cup the back of her neck. "Get over here."

"Seriously," she said, laughing. "I'm supposed to respond to 'get over here'?"

"If you want a kiss." He kept his eyes on the road, because he knew a curve was coming up. After that it was one mile to town.

She muttered something unintelligible and then slid closer. "It won't be much of a kiss with you driving," she murmured, the smile in her voice making him want to pull over and show her all kinds of things that could be done in the cab of a truck.

"You're right," he said. "We should forget it." Before she could mouth off, he slipped his hand from her shoulder to the top of her breast. "I like it better when you don't wear a bra."

Her sharp intake of breath pleased him. "That would've gone over well with your parents. Is that Blackfoot Falls coming up?"

"Yep." Lights glowed from Earl's filling station at the edge of town. Thank God. Noah's jeans were getting tight.

"We should stop in and check on Sadie."

"No stopping."

"But you're going to your office anyway."

"I lied."

Alana let out a short laugh. "Sheriff Calder."

He circled his thumb over her nipple, nice and hard even through the shirt and bra. "You have a problem with going straight home?"

"Not a one," she said breathlessly.

ALANA THOUGHT SHE HAD IT ALL planned out. As soon as they made it through the front door of his house, she was going to jump him and rip that damn shirt off. Screw the lead-up. Something could go wrong, like this morning, and she wasn't about to end up sleeping alone.

Ha.

The moment he had her inside, his mouth caught hers and he kicked the door closed behind them. *Guess he showed me,* she thought, and started giggling.

"What?"

"Lock it."

"I will."

"Now. I mean it," she said against his mouth, because he wouldn't stop kissing her. "I don't want any interruptions. And take the phone off the hook and turn off your cell."

That briefly brought him to a halt. "Sorry, the cell has to stay on." He flipped the lock on the door and then returned to nipping and sucking at her lips with an urgency that stole her breath.

He cupped her breast through the T-shirt, finding her hardened nipple and toying with it until a small whimper rose from her throat. She arched back and his other arm banded around her waist, pulling her tighter and closer until she gasped for air. Only then did he loosen his hold and yank the hem of her shirt from her Levi's.

She tried to get to his buttons, but he was in the way, pushing up her shirt and lowering his head to press soft kisses to the skin between her breasts. Alana didn't realize he'd un-snapped her bra until it slackened. He shoved aside the cups and rolled his tongue over one taut nipple, then drew it tightly into his mouth. Pleasure shimmered through her body and she clutched his shoulders, the feel of hard-muscled flesh beneath the soft cotton making her anxious to get at his buttons again.

He wasn't about to let her have her way. Maneuvering her past the recliner, then the couch, he kissed the line of her jaw, the side of her neck while he unsnapped her jeans. He steered her to the kitchen phone and used his elbow to knock the receiver from the cradle. The off-the-hook warning buzz startled her even though she should've expected it.

In the backyard, Dax started barking.

Noah cursed.

Alana laughed. "We have to let him in."

"I know," he muttered, and yanked down the tab of her zipper.

"You have a thing for kitchens?"

"Hmm?" He lifted his head and his mouth twisted in a lop-sided smile. "No, saving time. Jesus, Dax, shut up."

"I don't think he got that. Oh." She gasped at the warm, moist breath bathing her right breast. "Take off your shirt while I let him in."

"He's gonna be a pain in the ass," Noah murmured against her nipple, biting softly, then using his tongue to soothe.

"We'll give him a rawhide bone to keep him busy." She tried to move toward the back door, but Noah's growing fe-rocity overwhelmed her.

She was used to being more in charge, and she could barely breathe, much less order him to slow down. Probably because that wasn't what she wanted. She didn't want it to end, not the kisses, not the way he was reaching inside her waistband to rub her backside, or the way he suckled her as if he could never get enough. The bedroom—that would be good, though.

"Hey." She reached between them and touched his hard-on through the denim.

Noah groaned and took a shuddering breath.

She pressed her advantage, rubbing her palm up and down, delighting in the raspy moans coming from his throat. "We have to let Dax in before the neighbors start calling, or worse, knocking."

"You're right."

Just as she was about to turn to the door, he cupped her chin with his slightly callused hand and held her face still for a leisurely, heart-stopping kiss that said he wasn't done with her yet.

In the next couple minutes locks were checked, Dax was treated, twice, and the phone restored to order with the ringer turned off. Alana's jeans and heels and Noah's boots littered the hallway in their rush for his bedroom.

His comforter was still turned down from his nap. He had smoothed the brown sheets up to the pillows. The bed was king-size, and the four dark-wood bedposts inspired a fleeting but absurdly hot fantasy that had her swallowing hard. She spun toward him, her gaze going straight to the part of his chest where his shirt hung open.

Good Lord, he was perfect. He had plenty of lean muscle and there was a six-pack in there, but he wasn't one of those bulky, overly muscled guys.

"Why do I have less clothes on than you do?" she asked, grabbing his shirt and pulling him closer.

"I'm more determined."

"I doubt that."

"Yeah?" He had her T-shirt off in the space of two heartbeats. Another second and her bra was history.

Her shaky laugh ended in a shuddery sigh at the way his hungry gaze ran down her nearly nude body. He smiled at the pink panties, with which he was well acquainted, then slid a hand beneath the elastic.

"Hey, wait." She shoved ineffectually at him, trying to give herself enough room to finish stripping him.

"Did enough of that already." He kissed her hard, following her as she moved backward to the bed.

12

FLATTENING HER PALMS ON HIS chest, she pushed forcefully enough to show him she meant business. "Either I rip those jeans off or you do." She stared pointedly at the bulge behind his fly. It wouldn't be easy getting the zipper down, not without hurting him.

He shrugged out of his shirt and, biting her lip, she watched the muscles ripple and bunch across his shoulders.

She wanted to touch him, all of him, slowly…first with her fingertips and then her tongue. This was a new experience for Alana. She'd always assumed her appetite for sex was as healthy as the next woman's, but she knew better now. When it came to Noah, she was voracious.

He drew down his zipper, and the burning ache at the pit of her stomach spread lower until she had little choice but to fall back on the bed and squeeze her thighs together. Using her elbows and heels, she inched back while she watched him shuck off his jeans. He wore black boxers, but she already knew that—not the color, but this morning she'd felt enough of him to know he wasn't a briefs man.

"Take off your panties," he said, flinging his jeans at the dresser, his gaze practically devouring her.

"Take off your boxers."

With a deceptively cool smile curving his mouth, he bent over and finished undressing, and all she could think was, holy crap, she was in for a hell of a good night.

He didn't tell her again to remove her panties, but crawled in next to her and yanked them off. She thought she heard them tear. "Hey, you might've just messed up my whole week."

"I'll let you know when it's Sunday again," he said, and kissed the lower part of her belly. "Nice…"

"What?" She came up on her elbows and saw that he was referring to the small sculpted patch of hair. "Oh, it's a European wax," she said inanely, and then flopped back to roll her eyes at the ceiling.

"Good to know."

She felt his smile and then his teeth as he lightly bit the hypersensitive skin above the area in question, his seductively warm breath drifting lower, lower, stoking the burning ache between her thighs. He skimmed the curve of her hip, found her breast and teased the already rigid nipple, first with his fingers and then his tongue.

His earlier frenetic pace had slowed to languid petting, and she couldn't decide which she preferred. As long as he was touching her, she didn't care, she concluded, and arched into his mouth. He moved against her, his arousal heavy and hot on her outer thigh. The tingling started in her chest and radiated down to her belly. She clutched his arm, dug her fingers into his hard-muscled flesh. Not because she wanted him to stop; she wanted him to go on forever. But already the pressure was unmercifully building inside her and they'd barely gotten started. This was new, kind of crazy. Usually it took her ages to climax with a guy, but this cowboy had her on a hair trigger.

When he wedged his hand between her thighs she about flew off the mattress. "Condoms?" Her question was more a gasp than anything, and she tried to say it again, but he kept doing delicious things to her nipples.

He finally looked up long enough to say, "In my wallet." Then he went back to using his tongue in that clever way of his. And his fingers, God, his fingers...

"None in the nightstand?"

"I don't bring...no."

Her grip on his arm had to be painful, but she couldn't tell by him. "I'm your first?"

"Yeah, so be gentle with me."

She managed a shaky laugh, but decided not to tell him it was the other way around; she needed the TLC. "Not a chance."

"I figured." He used his teeth to lightly tug on her nipple, and she shuddered with pleasure.

"Condom. Now. Seriously."

He pulled back and gave her a considering look, his brow furrowed. "We'll use one. I'm not reckless—"

"No, it's not that.... I think we should have it nearby."

"Ah." One side of his mouth lifted, transforming his expression from mildly offended to pleased, and he rolled off the bed and retrieved his jeans.

She watched him remove his wallet, or rather she stared at his impressive hard-on and peripherally sensed everything else that was happening. If she'd thought the short time-out would help her cool down, was she ever wrong. Though if her gaze hadn't been glued to him the short break might've worked. He was stunning. Every part of him, his lean-muscled body, his chiseled face and those eyes...

Alana finally had to look away. She flipped onto her side and concentrated on plumping pillows, because if she kept looking at him, he'd just breathe on her and she'd come.

The mattress dipped behind her, and she felt his mouth at her lower back, pressing moist kisses until he got to her ass.

The first soft bite made her clench everything that would clench. He sure liked using his teeth, and who knew she'd love the sensation so much? She closed her eyes and gripped the pillow, letting him do whatever he was doing. In a second she'd reach behind and find his cock and—

She gasped. "Oh, my God, are you giving me a hickey?"

"I've never done that, not even when I was a kid." Sliding his hand between her thighs, he brushed his long fingers against her slick clit. "Why? You want one?"

Whimpering, she instinctively tried to squeeze her legs together, tried to twist around to face him, but he refused to move his hand. He glided his mouth along her spine until he got to her shoulder, his finger probing deeper, entering her and pushing inside until she whimpered again.

"You're so wet," he said, his voice hoarse and broken, almost a whisper. Without warning, he withdrew his hand and turned her over, pinning her back and shoulders to the mattress.

She stared up at him, mesmerized by the dark, sexy shade desire had turned his eyes, and felt her pulse hammering wildly at her throat. His gaze found the exact spot and then his head dipped as he pressed a kiss there.

When she reached between their bodies and touched him, he grunted, jerking back in surprise. She wrapped her fingers around him and slid her palm along the upward curve.

Noah's entire body shuddered and he made a deep sound of pleasure. "Jesus, I've got to get that condom on."

"You do," she said, enjoying the feel of him pulsing against her hand. She heard the packet tear, then smiled when he shoved her hand away.

"You're trying to kill me," he murmured.

"Hmm, pretty sure that's not the goal," she said, and wrapped her hand back around his cock.

His laugh came out tortured. He caught her chin and kissed

her hard on the mouth before trailing his lips to the skin below her ear. "I ought to give you a nice big hickey right here, a souvenir to take back to New York."

This time she did the shoving. "Don't you dare."

Grinning, he ducked away from her hand. "You know what happens when we start daring each other."

"Remind me."

Already sheathed, he positioned himself between her legs, and she sucked in a breath, heat swamping her, as she waited for him to enter her. His gaze on her face, he teased her with his fingers, sliding in and out, mimicking what he was about to do with his cock.

"Noah, please," she whispered.

He leaned down and kissed her, and then pulled her legs around his waist and pushed slow and deep inside her.

She let out a small moan, and he stopped, then eased back. "Don't," she said in a raw voice that couldn't be hers, and yet it was. "Don't stop."

He moved against her, shoving harder this time, faster, deeper. She bucked up to meet him, to show him she wanted him, all of him. And he eagerly delivered, filling her so completely that the room seemed to swim around her, making her dizzy, making her feel as if she would drown in all the heat. Her whole body trembled, as did his. The entire time he stared into her eyes, as if nothing else existed but the two of them, every move designed to ratchet up the tension until they were ready to ignite. Finally, he closed his eyes and held himself still, every muscle tight and straining. She climaxed so fiercely she almost didn't hear the cry that ripped from his throat.

The tears that filled her eyes defied explanation. She clung to him even as he collapsed against her, his chest heaving, his head resting heavily on her shoulder as he whispered her name.

NOAH WISHED HE COULD OPEN THE bedroom door a sliver to let in some light. Alana was curled up next to him, warm and naked, sound asleep, and he wanted to get a look at her. Wouldn't happen. For one thing, his arm was around her and her cheek was pressed to his shoulder. The other problem was Dax—if he heard anything and realized the door wasn't latched, he'd come bounding in and land on top of them before Noah could utter a word.

No, he'd let her sleep. It was the least he could do after keeping her up until one-thirty. Not that she'd complained. In fact, she'd been quite the eager and creative partner. Damn, the woman had him in a tailspin. One minute she reminded him of his former girlfriend in Chicago, driven and self-centered, and the next she was going out of her way to be kind to his mother, and stewing over Sadie.

Of course there was nothing wrong with being ambitious. He didn't want to be sheriff of Salina County forever. The job served his purpose for now. His parents weren't getting any younger, and the time was approaching when his father would be unable to refuse Noah's offer of paying someone to help with the ranch. The best solution would be to sell the small spread and move someplace that required less work, but he doubted that would be an option.

He was fairly certain his parents still lived in a dream world, thinking one of their children would end up taking over. His older sister and her husband would've been the most likely to keep the ranch in the family, maybe even expand the dinky operation, which had been increasingly neglected. But that wouldn't happen as long as their mother was still drinking.

Beside him, Alana stirred, sighing softly in her sleep and moving her hand to rest over his heart. He gazed down at her, and even though he couldn't see much in the darkness, he easily imagined how she'd looked a few hours ago in the glow of the lamplight, her hair mussed, her cheeks and nipples flushed as she straddled him and came for the third time.

He wished like hell he could get some movement on her stolen luggage. Aside from just giving her peace of mind and her life back, it would go a long way to making him feel as if he actually deserved being with her like this. What the hell good was a sheriff if he couldn't find a set of luggage and a purse in his own town? On the other hand, finding her things would mean there'd be no excuse for her to stay with him any longer. Though he'd like to think she'd stay anyway. Now that Noah had her in his bed, he wasn't willing to let her go until he had to.

As for his initial concern that she might be the grifter? He knew in his heart and his mind that she wasn't a criminal. It had just been a case of bad timing. And a son of a bitch who was bold enough to steal a woman's belongings in the middle of Main Street.

Noah shifted slightly, hoping to make her more comfortable. Wrong move. She jerked a little, her head coming up.

"Noah?" she said groggily.

"Shh. It's still early."

"What time is it?"

"Doesn't matter." He tucked her closer and stroked her hair, trying to coax her back to sleep.

She breathed in deeply and snuggled against him. "Do you have to work today?"

"Yep," he said regretfully. "I do."

Her disappointment came out in a heartfelt sigh.

He smiled and kissed the side of her forehead. Her hair caught on his chin, and he winced at the amount of rough stubble covering his jaw.

"Why aren't you asleep?" she asked, her fingers brushing his nipple. "You're the one who has to work."

"I only woke up a few minutes ago."

"Because I'm crowding you." She tried to move away, but he tightened his hold.

"Stay. I'll go back to sleep."

"Promise?"

"Promise."

With a contented purr, she drew closer again, her soft cheek pressed to his chest, her warm breath fanning his nipple, and dammit, his cock twitched. He wouldn't do anything about it, just keep still, wait to hear the low, even sound of her breathing. Then maybe he could turn his head and get a glimpse of the clock. For all he knew he had to be up in half an hour. Hard to tell this time of year. It was dark when he got out of bed and dark when he returned home in the evening.

Not today, though. Without compunction, he planned to cut out early and take her to the Sundance for a horseback ride and a few games of pool. After he called Rachel, of course, and explained what was what.

He'd known when he accepted the job that people would expect him to be available 24/7, that there would be some who'd want to deal only with him. That was the nature of being a small-town sheriff. But this week, the citizens of Salina County were gonna have to get used to calling the deputies. Because he had every intention of spending as much time as he could with Alana.

She shifted restlessly. "You're not sleeping," she whispered.

"Apparently, neither are you."

"What are we going to do about that?"

Smiling, he cupped her breast. Her nipple was already hard. He was halfway there himself. "Any ideas?"

She shivered against him. "I might have one," she said, sliding her palm down his belly.

"Oh, hell."

Her hand froze. "Um, okay."

"I just remembered. We used my last condom."

"You only had three?"

"Yep." Sighing with disgust, he stared glumly at the ceiling.

"Where do you usually buy them?"

"Not at Abe's or the Food Mart, that's for sure."

Alana lifted her head and grinned. "I bet everyone in town knows you've had sex already."

It struck him that enough light was seeping through the blinds that he could actually make out her face. He turned to glance at the clock. How could it be 7:20 already? "Sure, okay, let's go into Abe's together later and pick up a box."

She lost the smile, seemed to be considering the option, then said, "Ew."

Noah chuckled. "Tell me about it."

"Where do you go to buy them? The next town?"

"I don't recall. I've had quite a dry spell."

"Right," she drawled, and wrapped her fingers around his cock. "With all those cute young things staying at the Sundance? You should see the reviews…. Hey!" She squirmed, laughing and trying to fight off his marauding hand.

Damn reviews. They were downright embarrassing.

"Don't start something we can't finish," she warned, a sly smile tugging at her lips as she found his cock again.

"Plenty of things to do that won't require a condom." He nuzzled her neck, and her slight gasp reminded him how badly he needed a shave. "Sorry."

"No, don't stop."

He ran the pad of his thumb over her soft, pale skin. "I'll hurt you."

"I'm tough. I can take it."

Noah lifted the hair off her neck and gently rubbed her nape. She wasn't as tough as she thought she was. She could put on quite a show when she set her mind to it, and she didn't lack confidence, but tough…? "Actually, I have to get ready for work."

"No. Really?" She peered over him at the clock, affording him an enticing view of her breasts. "I thought it was the middle of the night."

He dipped his head for a taste. A swirl of his tongue, and she blossomed in his mouth. Wrong thing for him to do; in a minute it would be hell forcing himself out of bed, which would threaten his plans for later. Grudgingly, he lifted his head. "I'm coming home early. I thought we'd go out to the Sundance this afternoon."

"Why?" She blinked, then recoiled. "To get rid of me?"

So she'd had second thoughts about her vacation plans, too. "What do you think?" He slid a hand behind her neck and pulled her in for a long, leisurely kiss. When his cock got too interested, he broke off. "I want you to meet the McAllisters. They're like a second family to me. And I keep a horse there. Do you ride?"

She nodded. "Plus you said they have a pool table."

"You *are* a hustler."

She grinned and traced a seductive pattern on his chest with the tip of her finger. "And maybe one of the brothers has a few condoms you could borrow?"

Noah laughed. "Yep, thought of that, too."

"Good." She kissed his jaw, and he heard the rasp of her teeth against his stubble. "I'm tempted to keep you in bed, but I really want you home early."

He briefly closed his eyes when she kissed his right pec, then swiped her tongue across his nipple. So much for his resolve. "A few more minutes won't matter."

The words were barely out of his mouth when his cell phone rang.

"No way," Noah muttered, skimming a hand down her back.

"Could've been worse." She looked up with a resigned expression. "At least we weren't interrupted last night."

"There is that." He squeezed her ass, then rolled over and grabbed the phone off the nightstand. It was Roy. "What's up?"

"You alone, boss?" the deputy asked.

Noah frowned at the odd question, and swung his legs to the floor. "Yeah," he said, the hairs on the back of his neck standing. He sent Alana a smile of apology and headed out of the bedroom.

"I just got to the office and there was a fax waiting from Potter County. They caught the guy Moran was looking for outside of Billings."

"Good." Noah relaxed, stopping near the bathroom door to intercept Dax, who'd rounded the corner and was charging down the hall. "You didn't have to call for that."

"Yeah, I sorta did." He paused, clearing his throat. "The woman is still unaccounted for, but the guy confirmed they had a falling out and they split up late Thursday night. The jerk's a real prince. Left her stranded at a rest stop with only her purse, and now he's giving her up in exchange for leniency." Roy paused again. "The thing is, boss, he's pretty sure she was headed this way."

13

Noah felt as if he'd received a blow to his chest that knocked the air from his lungs. But the shock didn't last long. He stood by his instincts, but had to go by the book, anyway. "Okay," he said slowly, "so we still need to be on the lookout for her."

"Boss," Roy said, the reluctance in his voice akin to someone admitting to the dentist he needed a tooth pulled. "You gotta consider she might already be here."

Noah scrubbed his face, fully aware of what his deputy was getting at and how much he hated being the messenger. Did the whole friggin' town already know Noah had a thing for Alana?

What was wrong with him? Of course they did. And of course people were going to gossip, no matter what. The fact was, he needed to finish this investigation. There wasn't a choice involved.

He'd signed up for this. No matter that he knew better. He knew Alana. Her showing up was a coincidence. Not even that, because all kinds of women had been coming to stay at the Sundance. And the story about her stuff being stolen... There had been some thefts in the county....

He just had to figure out how she'd been robbed on Main Street with no one seeing a thing. It made no sense.

"Boss, you there?"

"Yeah." Noah grabbed Dax by the collar. "I'm trying to get this mutt out the back door." Buck naked, he half walked, half dragged the dog through the kitchen. "You talk to Gus or Danny yet?"

"Only Gus. So far none of the folks he's interviewed remember a thing, and he hasn't noticed any strange single women passing through. The Sundance guests show up in groups."

"She might not be alone. The woman's a con artist. We can't discount the possibility that she sweet-talked her way into hooking up with another guy." As he said that, alarm bells went off in Noah's head and his stomach turned. Jesus, was he being a sucker? No, he knew better. "I'll be in around eight. Hey, any chance the suspect they caught has a picture they can send us?"

"Sheriff Moran didn't say, but I'll give him a holler."

Noah disconnected the call and wrestled Dax outside. The dog wanted to be fed, and he would be in a minute. Noah had something else to do first, something he wished he didn't have to do.

Glancing at the clock, he quickly calculated the time in New York, then punched in the number for directory assistance. He paced to the hall while he waited, making sure Alana was still in the bedroom and couldn't hear him, and hoping like hell she had a landline in her name. She'd mentioned she had a housekeeper. Even if the woman didn't answer, hearing Alana's voicemail greeting would do a lot to ease his mind.

He found a listing for Alana Richardson in Manhattan and waited while the operator connected him. After the fourth ring, he expected to be switched to voicemail.

A woman answered.

He cupped a hand over his mouth and the receiver, while darting a glance toward the hall. "Alana Richardson, please."

"She's not here," the woman said. "This is her housekeeper. May I take a message for her?"

"Will Alana be back soon, or is she out of town?"

"Ms. Richardson will be away for the rest of the week," the woman said pleasantly. "She's in the Caribbean."

Noah took another look down the hall, as if that would help. "Are you sure?"

In response to his unintentionally harsh tone, there was a long pause, and he knew he wouldn't be getting any more information out of the woman. "May I ask who's calling?" She didn't sound friendly now.

"There's no message. Thanks." He disconnected the call and exhaled sharply, wondering what the hell that was about. There had to be a reasonable explanation, but it seemed as though Alana was determined to make his life as difficult as possible. Where the devil was her luggage?

His phone was set up to block his number and identity, not that he thought the housekeeper would be forthcoming with a Montana county sheriff. He toyed with the idea that Alana Richardson's identity had been stolen, but that didn't feel right, either. It was, however, possible.

Didn't mean he believed it.

Last night at supper with his parents...the conversation on their ride home...the intimacy they'd shared in his bed... nope. It was a mess, for sure, and he'd have to keep his mind open even when it was uncomfortable. But he was more determined than ever to get to the bottom of things. He'd been a damn good cop in Chicago, on a fast track to making detective, and he was a damn good sheriff. His gut had never let him down.

He listened for sounds from the bedroom. He couldn't hear anything—for all he knew she'd once more fallen asleep. But he didn't have to see or hear a thing. The knowledge that she was in his bed, naked, was enough to mess with his ability to think. What he needed to do was to get out of the house. Go to the office. Make sure his head was clear before he did anything else. He still had to talk to his other deputy, and the possibility that the suspect had avoided Blackfoot Falls was very real.

Coffee was tempting, but he decided he'd wait and get a cup at the office. No way around returning to the bedroom for his clothes before he jumped into the shower. Maybe he'd be lucky and she'd have gone back to sleep. Then he could leave her a note, because he just wasn't up to putting on his poker face.

He filled Dax's food bowl and left it outside the door. Before making the trip down the hall, he called Roy back. "I need you to do something for me," he told the deputy. "I'll be leaving here in about twenty minutes, but I want someone sitting on the house as soon as I leave."

After a telling silence, Roy said, "Huh?"

Noah had to smile. "You," he said, deciding not to bring in the other deputies on this one. "I want you to sit at the corner, not in a marked vehicle, but in your own truck, and watch the house. If Alana leaves, I want you to follow her."

"You mean tail her," he said excitedly.

"Yep, Roy, that's what I mean. Don't let her see you. Can you do that?"

"Sure, boss."

"And can you keep your mouth shut about this?"

"Who am I gonna tell?"

Noah let out an incredulous laugh.

Roy sniffed, making sure Noah knew he was offended. "I won't tell a soul."

"Not even Gus or Danny for now."

Roy hesitated, but didn't question the order. The deputy

loved to think he was Noah's right-hand man, and that inclination toward self-importance was what Noah was counting on to keep this quiet. "You got it. Where are you gonna be?"

"Working. Call my cell if there's anything to report. We clear?"

"Yep. I'll go bring my truck around. Wait…what if she tries to leave town?"

Noah winced at the thought. He plowed a hand through his hair and shook his head. "You call me. Then you stop her."

"Stop her. Right." Roy's voice cracked, and then he disconnected.

Noah went to get ready for work, certain his deputy was going to have a pretty boring day, undercover.

THE BRIGHT SUN WAS TRYING TO seep through the blinds. Noah's side of the bed was cold, and Alana knew he'd left. She wasn't sure how she knew, she just did. Still groggy, she squinted at the alarm clock. Seeing the red digital numbers spurred her awake. She'd never slept until ten-thirty in her life. Maybe when she was a kid, but she doubted Eleanor would have allowed such a thing even then.

Well, now Alana knew for sure Noah was gone. He would've let her sleep while he went to work, and she'd be surprised if he hadn't left her a note. Anxious to see what he'd written, she slipped out of bed, then checked the top of the dresser before pulling on a T-shirt and padding down the hall. She made a quick bathroom stop, the linoleum floor cold beneath her bare feet. Shuddering at her terrifying reflection in the mirror, she turned away and thought about collecting her stupid high heels from her room, because the kitchen floor would be equally cold. But she was too giddy over looking for his note. God, she'd never been this ridiculous, even in high school.

The piece of paper was on the kitchen counter next to the

coffeepot. It said he'd gone to work. He'd left his cell number if she needed him, and had signed it simply "Noah." Alana stared at the impersonal lines and wondered why that should hurt her. What had she expected? Or more to the point, had the right to expect? They had talked this morning, after all. And he was coming home early so they could go to the Sundance. Quite a concession for him, she suspected.

She studied the carefully printed phone number, tempted to call just to get a fix on his tone of voice. Reason won out and she set the note aside. She was being silly. He'd probably been late leaving for work, and she was lucky to have gotten a note at all. It was just that last night had been incredible, like nothing she'd ever experienced. Never had she let herself be swept away as she had with Noah.

Normally, she liked being in control, in every aspect of her life. It gave her comfort and security. But last night, God, all she'd ever known or thought she knew about herself be damned. Noah could've led her off the Brooklyn Bridge and she would have followed with bated breath. Right now she should be scared to death that she could be so weak. Instead, she watched the clock and calculated how many hours it would be before she'd see him again.

Oh, what the hell, this was her vacation—and a much better one than a stay at the dude ranch. Alana was allowed to be silly and fanciful. Five minutes back in her office and this would all go away. In a month, she'd barely remember Noah's name. Except damn, the man could kiss. Not to mention his other talents.

Shaking her head, she checked the coffeepot, smiling when she saw that he'd already measured out grounds and left water in the unit, ready for her to hit the on button. After getting it started, she heard Dax scratching at the door, and let him in. With big moon eyes, he gazed at the treat jar.

Alana laughed. "One. That's all you're getting." She fished

out a Milk-Bone, waited until he sat, and then held out the treat.

After he took it and scampered off, she got out a mug. Drumming her fingers on the counter, she watched the coffee drip into the carafe. It was going to take forever. She should probably shower while she waited. Although she was in no hurry, because except for a trip to the bank she didn't have a single thing to do today. Maybe after the Watering Hole opened she'd go check on Sadie. In the meantime, she could finish the book she'd started on Saturday.

Her eyes were drawn inexorably to the phone. She really, really wanted to call Noah. Not just to hear his voice, not at all. She had a perfectly good reason. If she knew when he planned on coming home, she could be ready. Maybe she could even have dinner waiting before they went to the Sundance. Snorting, she tapped the back of her head against an upper cabinet. Her, cook? That could end a perfectly terrific vacation fling very quickly.

Although she had made a passable quiche once in college...knowing Noah, if it didn't turn out, he'd appreciate the gesture. Alana opened the refrigerator and found he already had some of the ingredients. She'd have to pick up the rest; maybe she could do that on her way back from the bank this morning. She wished Noah could go with her, because she doubted the local bank had handled many wire transfers, and she'd probably have to wait for her money.

Her mind made up, she quickly showered and dressed, downed her coffee and debated borrowing the twenty-odd dollars Noah had left on his dresser. She still had a twenty from her pool winnings, but if the bank wouldn't release her funds right away she wanted to make sure she had enough to buy the things she needed. Deciding she should purchase extra ingredients in case the first quiche didn't turn out, she grabbed the money off his dresser, then headed to town.

NOAH CROUCHED DOWN CLOSE TO where the wire had been cut from Cy Heber's fence and inspected the faint tread marks in the hard dirt. No cattle were missing, because Cy had heard something early that morning and come running out with his shotgun. But the old man was right—someone had been up to no good out here. No telling what might've happened if Cy hadn't been battling insomnia.

"You hired any help lately?" Noah asked, standing.

"Nope. Can't afford it. You want coffee? Shirley just made a fresh pot."

"Yeah, I'll take a cup. Thanks." Noah watched the stooped older man turn and limp toward the small clapboard ranch house. "And leave the rifle inside."

Cy didn't turn around, but raised a hand as he kept walking, acknowledging he'd heard.

The guy had been making Noah nervous, waving that Winchester around. Not that he blamed the old-timer for being guarded. He and Shirley were pretty isolated this far east of Blackfoot Falls. That was part of what made this alleged robbery attempt so puzzling. Someone had to be real familiar with the area to know the Hebers were out here. And hell, they didn't even have that much stock.

Noah's cell rang, and before he answered, he saw that it was Roy.

"I'm sorry, boss. I lost her."

"What do you mean, you lost her?"

"I did just like you told me. I sat in my truck, watched her come out of your house and walk to the bank. I kept waiting and waiting, and when she didn't come out, I went inside. Real calm like, as if I was doing personal business and—"

"Roy." Noah's patience slipped. "The bottom line."

"Herman told me she asked him to call her bank in New York City. The fella on the other end knew who she was right away, and they're sending her money. A lot of money."

That was good news. Noah relaxed a little.

"After that, she left, didn't say where she was going. I swear I was watching the door the whole time. I didn't look down once at my new *Sports Illustrated*."

Jesus. "Go check the Watering Hole. She might be with Sadie. Call me back." He started to slip the cell into his pocket, but for the hell of it, called his home phone. No answer. He hadn't expected her to be there, but he was relieved that she'd had no problem at the bank. The housekeeper thing still bothered him, though....

Cy returned with a mug of coffee for each of them, and Noah tried his best to keep his focus on their conversation. But his thoughts kept drifting back to Alana and Roy, and why there'd been no call assuring him she had gone to the Watering Hole. When Cy asked him to help mend the cut fence, Noah agreed. His job, including fence mending, came first.

A READY-MADE PIE CRUST would've solved so much of Alana's problem. However, she'd learned that the Food Mart had never carried such an item, and the manager couldn't imagine why they ever would. After all, a pie crust was one of the easiest things in the world to whip together.

Yeah, and Alana really loved being patronized by a smiling, pimply-faced twenty-year-old who'd probably majored in Home Economics, if the schools still had such a horrifying option as part of their curriculum.

Sighing, Alana used the back of her wrist to wipe the flour off her nose. It wasn't the poor woman's fault she still had acne problems, and Alana felt duly ashamed for the mean thought. But that wasn't going to help her pathetic quiche. She doubted starting over for the third time would do any good, either.

Crap, she was just too much of a perfectionist, she decided, tilting her head and eyeing the lopsided baked crust. So what if it was uneven. Most of it would be hidden by the filling, and who the hell had thought up fluted edges, anyway?

Her decision made, she poured the egg, spinach and mushroom mixture into the crust. The oven was already heated, so she opened the door and slid in the quiche. She heard Dax bark at the back door and felt badly for making him go outside on such a chilly day, but he'd kept getting underfoot.

She set the timer, then grabbed a treat from the jar and headed out to join him. Even though she still hadn't forgiven the mutt for turning his nose up at the proffered piece of crust from her first attempt.

It was the middle of the afternoon, the air crisp and the sky a beautiful clear blue. The mountaintops in the distance were already capped in white, and she tried to imagine what the place would look like covered with a pristine blanket of fresh snow instead of the slushy gray stuff she was used to in New York. Oh, the snow always looked pretty when it first came down on Manhattan, but it didn't take long for the plows and taxis to push everything into depressing heaps against the curbs.

Dax left her sitting at the picnic table and ran to the kitchen door, barking. Was someone knocking? She hadn't heard a car. Could be Noah, though she hadn't expected him this early. Her pulse quickening, she sprang to her feet. God, she was going to have to break down and buy some sensible shoes. Or maybe even a pair of Western boots. She would never wear them again, but had to have something besides these unsuitable heels. She'd started losing hope her luggage would ever be recovered.

Blocking Dax's entrance, she slowly opened the door. A creepy feeling slithered up her spine. The house seemed eerily quiet, and reconsidering, she let the dog in ahead of her. He took off into the living room, and the barking stopped.

"Noah?"

No answer.

She entered the living room, craning her neck to see if his truck was parked in front.

"Alana." Noah appeared from the hall, and she nearly jumped out of her jeans. "You're here."

"I'm here," she confirmed, laughing nervously, her hand at her throat. "Where else would I be?"

"I heard you went to the bank. If they wired your money, then you'd be free to skip town."

"What?" She laughed. "Why would I do that?"

He seemed to relax, putting his hands on his hips and shaking his head. "What does a woman like you want with a small-town sheriff like me?" He smiled, but there was still something troubling about the way he looked at her...and that he hadn't kissed her yet.

She thought about the note he'd left her, how it hadn't even sounded like him. Did he really think she would ditch him the minute the money came through?

"What's got into you?" she asked uneasily. He was too confident a man to be that insecure. More importantly, she'd believed last night had meant something to both of them.... A thought struck her. He'd just come from his room. Probably noticed the money was missing from his dresser.

"For God's sake, I'm going to pay you back. The bank will be releasing my funds later this afternoon or first thing tomorrow morning. I needed something from the grocery—" To her horror, her voice cracked. Emotion swelled in her throat. She didn't have to take this crap. "Forget it. Okay? Just forget it. The minute my funds clear, I'll be out of your hair."

"Alana." His arm shot out to stop her when she tried to make it past him, but she jerked out of his reach.

If she could just get to her room, lock the door, not come out until the bank called. Or better yet, crawl out the window so she didn't have to see him. He knew she'd gotten choked up, and that pissed her off.

"Would you please wait?" He caught her from behind, pulling her back against his chest.

She tried to pry his arm away, but it was like a steel band around her waist, trapping her body snugly to his. "Let go of me."

"We need to talk."

"I'll scream."

"No, you won't." His lips brushed the side of her neck, his moist breath tickling her ear.

"I will," she said, and would've sounded so much more convincing if she'd been able to breathe. She could blame the tightness of his arm under her breasts, but that would be a lie. He'd loosened his hold, and she was staying pressed against his chest of her own volition.

"I'm sorry, sweetheart," he whispered. She should've torn his head off for using the term, but coming from him she actually liked it.

"I've just had one hell of a day. I don't have any problem with you borrowing—" His abrupt retreat left her reeling. "Something's burning."

"Burning?" She spun around to look at him, her brow furrowed. Then her eyes widened. "Oh, God." She pushed past him and ran to the kitchen.

He followed, watched her pick up a dish towel and open the oven. Smoke drifted out, but not enough to make him grab the fire extinguisher. The acrid smell seemed to be the worst of it. She coughed and backed away, waving furiously at the smoky air.

"You okay?" He drew her toward him, turned off the oven and used the toe of his boot to shut the door.

"It's not the quiche. I mean, it is, but not the one baking

now, because it hasn't been in long enough." Her shoulders slumped. "I think the smoke is from a spill from my first attempt." She sighed. "But now our dinner isn't finished and I don't know what to do about it. I'll have to wait for the oven to cool in order to clean it."

"Quiche?" He'd tried it once. That was enough.

She studied his face. "I knew I was taking a chance that you wouldn't like it, but that's all I know how to make."

He tried to control a smile. Obviously she wasn't an ace at quiche, either. Fine with him. "We're going to remove the pan, let the oven cool, then go from there."

"All right." She picked up the dish towel again and inhaled deeply, as if bracing herself for the ordeal of opening the oven once more.

"Here." He took the towel from her and did the honors. Then frowned at the sunken blob in the pan he put on the stove. He thought he knew what quiche was, but this wasn't what he remembered.

"What happened?" Alana was staring at it, too.

"Beats me."

"I think I put in too much cream the second time. Or did I forget the eggs?" She bent to peek into the oven, then abruptly straightened with a look of dread on her face. "I'll have money soon. Anyone you think will do it…I'll pay them a hundred dollars to clean that oven."

Noah chuckled. "It's a newer model, so it's got a self-cleaning feature."

She flushed. "I'm really a very capable advertising executive. I am, I swear. Some ads you see on TV—the man in the polo shirt on a horse, the razors and shirtless guys? That's me. I thought of those." She made a little sound of exasperation and looked so miserable that he sucked up a laugh. "This kind of stuff…" She spread a hand. "I'm not so good."

He discreetly wiped the smudge of flour dusting her jaw

by finger-combing her hair back from her face. Her cheeks were warm, still flushed, her eyes a soft chocolate-brown. She looked beautiful. "I came home to sweep you off your feet and make mad passionate love to you, but now I don't know...." He shook his head. "A woman who doesn't know how to make quiche? I'm thinking, deal breaker."

She gave him a wry smile. "That's not why you came home."

"You doubt me, woman?"

Her warning glare didn't quite come off. "Oh." She put her hands on his shoulders, and he placed his at her waist. "Don't think I didn't hear you call me sweetheart."

"Ah, right, sorry. Won't let it happen again." He winked. "At least I'll try not to."

Smiling, she slipped her arms around his neck and sniffed. "You smell like smoke."

"You're not smelling like a rose yourself."

Her grin widened. "We could take a shower together."

Dammit, he still had to go to the office, and though he said nothing, he could see by the disappointment that flickered in her eyes that she knew he couldn't stay.

"It's okay," she said gamely, "I understand. You're still working."

"I have to write a report." Sliding his arms around her, he lifted her off the floor and kissed her soft lips. They eagerly parted for him, and he knew he was in trouble.

Only twenty minutes ago he'd walked into the house, tired and cranky and full of doubt. He'd expected that she'd left town right under his deputy's nose, but not because she was a con artist.

A few minutes under her spell and he was back to appreciating how lucky he was to have found Alana, even if it was just for a little while.

14

ONCE THE OVEN WAS SET TO self-clean, there wasn't a whole lot for Alana to do except obsess over every single word Noah had said before he'd gone back to work. Which she refused to do. She wasn't fifteen, she wasn't writing "Mrs. Alana Calder" in her notebooks, and God, she barely could believe she'd let herself come to this over a man. Over a small-time sheriff.

It had to be the water.

Clearly, what she needed to do was get out of the house.

She'd go to the bank to check on the money, then to the Watering Hole to look in on Sadie. Alana was strongly considering having herself that cosmo she'd wanted on day one.

Dax barked when she left, which probably put the whole town on alert, but even Noah couldn't believe they were anything close to a secret anymore. Alana had grown so used to the anonymity of Manhattan that she barely thought about it. She knew the names of the doormen and her immediate neighbors. Other than that, all her acquaintances were useful. The maître d' at Per Se, her hairdresser, the assistants who worked for her important clients. It boggled her mind that you could know every person in a town. Know their history, their secrets.

Frankly, she was surprised there weren't a lot more crimes of passion in small communities.

It didn't take her long to hit the center of town. Tempted to stop in to see Noah at the sheriff's office, she purposely headed for the bank. Three steps later, she heard a familiar voice behind her.

"Still here? Oh, that's right. I heard you were shackin' up with Calder. The Sundance ought to change its name to Whorehouse."

Stunned speechless, Alana spun around, suddenly steady on her four-inch heels. It was Gunderson, of course; she'd have recognized that weasel's voice if she'd run into him in Times Square. "What did you say?"

"You heard me."

The man who'd been so put together the other day had apparently been drinking. It wasn't obvious, but he was leaning against a big truck that she doubted was his. It wasn't fancy enough. Although, was that Tony in the front seat?

She didn't have to wonder for long, because the passenger door opened, and sure enough, the stocky kid who'd just turned twenty-one stepped onto the street. Behind him, another big guy slammed the back door shut. The two of them looked like football players. But she was more interested in Gunderson.

"That's quite a mouth you've got there," she said. "You in the habit of spitting out that kind of accusation when you don't have one fact to go on?"

"I've got all the evidence I need. I saw you come out of his house."

"Funny how you managed to see me leaving a house down the street and around the corner, but you couldn't see a person directly behind me steal my luggage."

The two husky kids, cowboy hats low on their foreheads, shirts stuffed with muscles, took a step closer to their boss.

Tony looked around, stalling when his gaze fell on Abe's Variety.

"You're crazy," Gunderson said, wiping a hand across his mouth. "You made up that story."

"You're a bald-faced liar, Gunderson. And you know it." She said the words calmly, but firmly. The man was a pig. What she couldn't understand was why people in this town were so afraid of him.

"And you think *I've* got a mouth," he said, only now he was speaking low and close, even if they were at least ten feet apart. "You don't come into my town and call me a liar. Not if you know what's good for you."

"Is that a threat?"

Gunderson opened his mouth, but before he could get the next word out, another voice interjected. "What the hell's got into you, Gunderson?"

Alana felt the tight knot that had gripped her stomach ease up as soon as she heard Noah. How long had he been listening? Surely he hadn't witnessed the opening volley, or he'd have been at her side in seconds.

"I'm thinking you'd better be gettin' on home," Noah said, approaching the old man. "You're not looking well."

Gunderson seemed ready to argue, but he ended up staring at Noah for what felt like a long time. Then he swiped his hand through the air as if he was finished with the whole business. His boys picked up his signal fast, Tony walking him straight to the front passenger seat. The other one got behind the wheel, and in a moment they'd driven off, leaving Alana buzzing with frustration.

Noah was staring after the truck. Across the way a woman Alana hadn't seen before was standing stock-still, holding on to her restless child's hand.

When Alana turned toward the Watering Hole, she saw two

other people, a man and a woman, gazing at her as if they'd never seen such a sight.

"What was that about?" Noah asked, touching the back of her arm.

"All I know is that he is one horrible man. I don't care if he is drunk, that was...that was abhorrent. I've never had anyone speak to me like that before."

"What did he say?"

Of course Noah hadn't heard the worst of it. She doubted there was any reason to be specific. She didn't need him getting worked up, not on that bastard's account. "He cast aspersions on the McAllisters ranch and their guests. *And* he denied having seen the thief who stole my things. Again. Dammit, he was right in front of me. There's no way he didn't see what happened."

Noah stepped closer to her. "I believe you," he said, lowering his voice, marking the conversation as private despite the fact that there were four people watching. "Let's talk it through inside. I want to hear everything he said."

NOAH COULD SEE SHE WASN'T happy with his suggestion. Her cheeks were pink; her eyes dilated. Her movements were jerky, her body obviously filled with adrenaline and righteous anger. Tough. He wasn't happy with her right now, either.

"You did question him, right?" she asked. "You said you were going to."

"Didn't I tell you I'd handle it?"

She blinked at his gruff tone. "Sorry," she murmured. "But you had to know he wasn't telling you the truth."

"Alana. I have no proof. It's your word against his."

The way she looked at him made Noah's gut tighten. It was as if he'd disappointed her on purpose. He felt like the most incompetent sheriff in the country, and all because of a pair of accusing brown eyes. Didn't mean he wasn't still pissed.

He didn't need her shooting her mouth off in front of everyone. She might be good at her job, but so was he.

Standing out here wasn't helping anyone, though. "Let's go back to the house. Have some coffee. Talk it through. Maybe there's something we overlooked, some little thing that seemed inconsequential but might not be."

She seemed to deflate, as if someone let all the life out of her like air from a balloon. "Fine. I can call the bank. I was just killing time until you got off work."

He pulled his cell out of his pocket and pressed speed dial for Roy. As soon as his deputy answered he said, "Take over, will ya?"

"You bet, boss."

Noah disconnected and walked her down the street toward privacy. With every step, the gap between them widened. She had been on fire facing Gunderson, her back straight, her intention to decimate the old man clear. It filled Noah with alarm, because he should have been there to stop things before they got started. But there was also part of him that wanted to shake her. If those mixed feelings weren't screwed up enough, he'd also experienced a weird kind of pride in her strength.

It wasn't just the loss of her personal belongings that had her making quiches and wearing Sunday panties. She might as well have landed on the moon. Blackfoot Falls wasn't big enough for the likes of Alana Richardson. New York barely was.

She sure as hell wouldn't ever be satisfied with a two-bit lawman like him. He was the very definition of a vacation fling. The minute she saw this town in the rearview mirror, he'd be a minor footnote never to be looked at again.

Noah wasn't sure why that hurt as much as it did, especially considering he hadn't ever thought of her as someone to keep.

After closing the door behind them, he led her into the kitchen and started preparing a new pot of coffee.

She sat down and stared at the wall.

"You want to take me through it?" he asked.

"No."

He stopped counting scoops and turned to her. "Why not?"

"His word against mine." She met his gaze. "I told you everything. The theft took less than a minute. I didn't leave a single detail out. If you can't find a witness, there's nothing left to do. It's as simple as that. Once I have money, I'll figure out a way to replace my ID so I can catch my plane home. It's all pretty simple, really. And for the record, I am sorry. I didn't mean to step on your toes by getting into it with Gunderson."

"Alana—"

"It's okay," she said. She took in a breath, then let it out, and by the time she inhaled again, she was smiling a little. "It's more than okay." She stood up and walked to him. "Weighing the two things, I think I've come out ahead."

"You lost me. What two things?"

"Losing my luggage. Meeting you."

He slid a gaze over her face, down the front of her shirt, then returned to her eyes. Dammit, he wasn't going to ruin the time they had left. He abandoned the coffee for a much better idea. Taking her hand in his, he led her out of the kitchen into the living room. He meant to head straight back to the bedroom, but she bumped her hip against his, and that stopped him. But only for a moment as he went for his buttons. "Have I mentioned that you look nice?" He stripped off his uniform shirt and threw it on the couch.

ALANA BLINKED. "WHAT ARE YOU doing?" Something was different about him. Different from when he'd been home earlier. Different from a few minutes ago. He seemed totally relaxed, yet full of purpose. Every ounce of his attention was on her and nothing else. This was the man who'd nearly had her begging last night. "What's gotten into you?"

"Despite a few rough patches, today is turning out to be pretty damn sweet."

"I'm happy for you. And in a minute, the rest of the block is going to be thrilled." She nodded past him with her chin. "The curtains are open."

He unsnapped his jeans, then nonchalantly pulled the curtains shut, while she decided to go with the flow. She hadn't lied to him. He was the best vacation she'd ever had, and she'd do it all again. Except she'd have worn more comfortable shoes.

Damn, he had a great chest. Perfectly defined back. Broad where he should be, narrow where he shouldn't. And his butt… She swallowed, her mouth suddenly dry. "You trying to get out of eating that quiche?"

"I'm in the mood for something else," he said, advancing toward her slowly.

Excited to see what he'd do, she didn't move. Just stood there, unsteady from her heart slamming against her breastbone, and growing damp between her thighs.

He stopped in front of her and nudged her chin up. "You're short without those heels."

She could argue the point, but she had something else in mind. Raising herself on tiptoes, she bit the tip of his chin, the feel of his slight stubble sending a shiver down her spine.

Noah's mouth brushed hers, and then he slanted his head and kissed her gently, so gently that she wasn't aware he'd teased her lips open until his tongue touched hers. He swept inside, tasting and probing, while he unfastened her Levi's. They were a size too big, and with a couple of wiggles the jeans fell to her ankles. She stepped out of them as he pulled off her T-shirt.

Her breath caught when he reached inside her panties. She instinctively squeezed her thighs together, but he'd already slid his fingers between her lips. "We're standing in the living room," she said, clutching at his arm.

"Jesus, you're so wet." His voice came out in a ragged breath. "Take off your bra."

"We should go—"

"Please."

The tone of his voice made her quickly unfasten the clasp. Pushing back her shoulders, she let the bra fall to the floor behind her. He entered her with two fingers, and she bucked against his hand.

He kissed her hard and drove in deeper, while rubbing her sweet spot with his thumb. She didn't know how much longer she could stand there—her knees were weak, her legs starting to wobble. Abruptly, he withdrew. A whimper of loss had barely escaped her when he scooped her up in his arms and carried her to the couch.

Laying her gently against the cool leather, he followed her down, teasing one breast, then the other while he pulled off her panties.

"Your jeans…" she whispered.

"Not yet."

Now it was her turn. "Please."

He didn't comply, only lifted his head, his mouth curved in a sly smile full of wicked intentions. It should have infuriated her, but all she wanted to do was beg. Plead with him to get naked and stretch his body over hers, push himself inside her.

Alana gasped. "Did you get condoms?"

His eyes briefly closed and he shook his head. "We won't do anything risky."

"But I want you inside me," she said softly, miserably aware that she sounded like a petulant child.

"Trust me." Holding her gaze, he ran his palm over her hip,

down the side of her leg, and then circled his hand around her ankle and brought it to his lips.

He kissed the inside, then worked his way to her knee and onward, pressing his hot damp mouth to the sensitive skin of her inner thigh. She tensed, and he finally broke eye contact to focus on what he was doing to her.

For a few seconds, shyness suffused her in a warm flush she seemed helpless to stop. Totally atypical for Alana, but then she'd never had a man stare at her in the bold, sexy way Noah was as he coaxed her lips apart.

He brushed his fingers over her, then raised his gaze to hers again. "Don't look so worried."

"I'm not…I'm just…" She breathed in deeply and managed to smile. "I'm not." She could scarcely explain that she'd never been with a man like him before, not even in college during her short rebellious streak.

The guys she'd been with were more like her—daring enough but not too reckless, smart, armed with an Ivy League education and certainty about their future. They'd probably turned out like the men she occasionally dated now, with their expensive haircuts, designer suits, enough assets to subsidize Brooklyn. When the pricey clothes came off, sex was okay, but sleeping with those men was never anything spectacular.

Now that she thought about it, sex was more like a polite business deal—short, civilized, to the point. But with Noah?

Looking into his handsome face, those smoky blue-green eyes that were too sexy for his or her own good, Alana found her entire body trembling. He was just so damn…male, and much more physical than she was used to. He didn't hesitate to take what he wanted from an amenable partner.

And confidence? Good God, he had that to spare, whether he was wearing worn jeans or nothing at all. Without question he was the one in charge, and that should've irritated her, maybe even thrown her off track a bit. Definitely not turned her on, made her ache and burn so hot she thought she was losing her mind.

He stroked between her thighs and lazily met her gaze. Those eyes alone could make a woman fear she'd teetered too close to the edge. That one misstep could bring doom.

"Sure wish I knew what you were thinking," he said, his lips quirking in a slow smile.

"Right now my brain is mush."

"Mush is good." He put his mouth on her, and she arched off the couch, gasping.

While he used his tongue and teeth to drive her crazy, he cupped a breast and kneaded the sensitive flesh. Her nipple was unbearably tender, so she flinched a little. His fingers stilled, withdrew.

Alana pulled on his forearm and forced his hand back to her breast. Felt his smile blossom against her, then the long glide of his tongue, which made her shudder.

The sensation was like an electrical current. She grabbed the back of the couch, disoriented, surprised that she was coming so quickly, shocked at the intensity of the climax that broke over her in wave after unrelenting wave. Instinctively, she tried to get away, evade his insistent tongue, but he had a firm grip of her hips, and she convulsed again, over and over, until she thought she just might die from it.

Noah was breathing hard when he finally lifted his head, his mouth damp, his nostrils flaring, his eyes nearly black. And his chest—his strong, broad chest with its light sheen of sweat—heaved with every deep breath he drew. God, how she wanted him inside her. This so wasn't fair.

"Come here," she whispered, opening her arms to him.

"No."

"Noah." She lowered her gaze to the swell of his fly and threw his own words back at him. "Trust me."

He caught her hand, kissed her palm. "We'll go get condoms."

"Yes, later." She curled up to a half-sitting position, and with her free hand rubbed his fly.

"Jesus, don't."

"Take off your jeans."

His hooded eyes were practically slits. "Alana…"

"Do it."

His big body shuddered and he slowly did as she asked. He pushed the jeans down his lean hips, and freed from the denim, his arousal thrust into her waiting hand.

"SHE'S GONNA WHIP YOUR ASS again, Calder." Leaning against the wood-paneled wall and grinning, Trace McAllister tipped a bottle of beer to his lips.

Noah scoffed. "I let her win the first game."

Cole and Rachel laughed. They were brother and sister, but couldn't have looked more different. Cole had dark hair and dark eyes, while Rachel was fair-skinned with a thick auburn mane and green eyes. Then there was Trace with his brother's sable-brown hair and eyes like his sister's.

Alana hadn't met Jesse, the middle brother, yet, or their mother, but she had a feeling she'd like them as much as she did these three. Fifteen minutes after she and Noah had arrived at the Sundance, she'd felt as if she'd known them forever. Rachel had apologized profusely for the mix-up with the reservations, which was nice, but not necessary. Alana hadn't missed the curiosity on all their faces, which she'd expected. But they couldn't have made her feel more welcome.

Three guests of the ranch had been sitting on the porch of the large house, bantering with the hands, when she and Noah had driven up in his truck. The women's stunned glares watching him take her hand weren't unexpected, either, but Alana had enjoyed that. She'd nudged him and asked if she was supposed to be his bodyguard. He'd only grunted, then given her one of those sexy looks that said he'd make her pay for that remark later. Worked for her.

She watched Noah line up his shot now, and sincerely hoped that he did win this one. Letting him beat her wasn't an option. He'd know and he wouldn't like it.

Sitting on the comfy black leather couch near the fireplace, Rachel waited until Noah pocketed the six ball and said, "Sorry, guys, I have to go make nice with our guests. I should've asked, though, have you eaten yet?"

"Yep," Noah said with a straight face. "We had quiche."

Trace snorted. "You had what?"

"Quiche." Noah repeated the lie and met her eyes, his filled with devilish amusement.

Cole rubbed the back of his head and tried to hide a smile.

Rachel didn't hold back. After a good chuckle, she asked, "Does that mean you want leftovers? We had pot roast."

"Yes, ma'am. Bag 'er up." Noah took another shot and missed, then muttered under his breath.

"I'm out for blood now, mister." Alana patted him on the butt as she slipped around him to gauge her next move.

Rachel had already walked out of the room, but Alana didn't miss the look that passed between the two brothers. She didn't care what they thought, only because it clearly didn't matter to Noah. Cole was his best friend.

In fact, he was the keeper of the condoms. That was the main reason she'd agreed to get dressed and come to the Sundance, or else she might've been tempted to handcuff Noah to the couch. But now she was really glad she'd come. She loved meeting his friends and seeing how the McAllisters served as a second family to him. He was so comfortable around them, and so was she. It made her a little sad that she didn't have anyone like them back in New York. Her fault entirely for focusing all her attention on work, but still.

She leaned over the table, lining up the fifteen, and sensed Noah behind her. Not touching her, but he was there; she confirmed it with a glance over her shoulder. "What are you doing?"

"Nothing." He checked out her ass, then raised his gaze and gave her an innocent smile.

Trace laughed. "I hope you wipe the floor with him. The bastard always beats me two out of three and I'm damn good."

Alana darted another look at Noah. Maybe she was the one being played.

"There you are." A pretty brunette stuck her head in and smiled at Trace. "I thought I heard your voice. You ready?"

His confused expression gave way to awareness. Whatever they had planned, he'd obviously forgotten. "Be right there." He waited until she left, and muttered, "Hell," then drained his beer and headed toward the door. "Nice meeting you, Alana."

After he'd disappeared, Noah grinned at Cole. "The kid's still burning the midnight oil?"

"He's cooled it some. If Rachel closed shop for the winter, it would be fine with him. Maybe he'd get some rest."

"You could all use the break, I suspect," Noah said, and Cole seemed hesitant to react, probably because Alana was supposed to have been a guest. "At least you met Jamie. Is she coming back for the holidays, or are you going to L.A.?"

Pretending she wasn't listening, Alana took her shot and missed by the skin of her teeth. She wanted to know who Jamie was, but decided she'd ask Noah privately. She wasn't even sure why she cared. This thing between her and Noah was a one-off. What happened here in Montana would stay in Montana. Forever. There was no other way.

She swallowed around the sudden lump in her throat, and

stood back for him to take his turn. The bastard ran the rest of the table without a single pause between shots, except to wink at her.

15

LATE WEDNESDAY MORNING, WHILE Noah was working, Alana walked over to the Watering Hole to visit Sadie. The bar wasn't open yet, but Sadie was putting up last-minute Halloween decorations, and Alana had promised to give her a hand.

"Hello, stranger," she said when she opened the door. "Hurry on in before the booze hounds come sniffing around, trying to get me to open early."

Alana glanced over her shoulder. "Who?"

"Avery and his sidekick. Gotten so I hate seeing his dilapidated rust bucket coming down Main. The old buzzard does nothing but complain ever since the Sundance opened." Sadie turned the dead bolt, then walked ahead, her limp noticeably improved. "Heard you were out there with Noah on Monday."

Alana shook her head. The Blackfoot Falls rumor mill was truly impressive. "We were, and I met the McAllisters. They were great. Although I didn't meet Jesse or their mother. Your leg seems better."

"Yep, saw the doc today and even he thinks there's hope for me yet." Sadie grinned and slid her bulk onto a stool at the bar in front of a box of decorations. "I also heard you stopped in here Monday, checking up on me."

"I was very pleased to hear you took time off to rest your

leg." Alana peered into the box before taking the stool next to Sadie. "You're starting late. Halloween is in, what, two, three days?"

"I wasn't gonna bother. If people wanna drink, they'll come. They won't care if I've draped crepe paper around the bar and hung tacky ghosts from the ceiling."

Alana figured she was past the danger point. If Sadie had intended to bring up her shouting match with Gunderson, she would have already. So Alana just smiled. "What changed your mind?"

"I was talking to Marge over at the diner and she thinks I'm being shortsighted. With the Sundance bringing in tourists, and Clyde who owns the Double R and Eli Roscoe from the Circle K talking about following in their footsteps, Marge thinks we should do more to spruce up the town. Maybe keep the boys from taking those gals to Kalispell or anyplace else."

"You mean others ranchers are thinking of switching to dude ranches?"

"Nah, they wouldn't out-and-out change over. They're mostly cattlemen. But a lot of people have large houses, or bunkhouses they don't use anymore, that they could convert to guest quarters and start their own dude ranches. With the price of corn, this area's been hurt bad. People gotta do whatever they have to do to survive." Sadie pulled out a roll of black crepe paper from the box, her dark brows dipped in a frown. "Even with the likes of Avery Phelps shooting his mouth off about strangers bringing nothing but trouble."

"Any truth to that?"

Sadie snorted and waved a plump hand. "Not a lick. I feel sorry for the man. His wife died, and he's been miserable ever since, but it wasn't like he treated her so good when she was alive, either. Now it seems all he does is drink and try to make everyone else as miserable as him. That's the reason he's taken up with Gunderson. They used to hate each other, now they're like two peas in a pod, trying to rile the McAllisters."

Alana's attention sharpened at the mention of Gunderson. "What's the deal with him, anyway? Why does everyone tiptoe around him?"

"Hmm, ornery old bastard is the richest man in the county," Sadie said. "He wouldn't personally have anything to do with stealing your things, but I wouldn't put it past him to keep his mouth shut if he saw who did. Probably figured you were a Sundance guest and decided to let the feathers fly." She rooted around inside the box, then flapped her hand at the airborne dust she'd stirred up. "It's not as if he doesn't have enough land, but he's been trying to get the McAllisters to sell him a piece of their spread for over forty years. I suspect they might've had to cave in until Rachel started bringing in money with her dude ranch idea."

"I'm sorry it's been that bad for them," Alana said quietly. Glancing around the bar, she was suddenly aware that the wood-plank floor and rickety stools that she'd assumed were intentionally rustic actually were in need of repair.

"Like it or not, the town has benefited from the McAllisters' gumption," Sadie said.

Alana inhaled deeply. "Then let's keep the tourists and their money right here in Blackfoot Falls."

The woman's eyebrows rose. "What's that?"

"Don't give them a reason to drive to Kalispell or wherever." Excited, with ideas already starting to flow, Alana slipped off her stool and started walking around the tables. "You have extra room here—who owns that vacant space next door?"

"I do."

"Fantastic." She knocked on the dividing wall. "There's no brick behind here, is there?"

"Girl, what are you doing?"

"What would you think about turning the Watering Hole into an old-time saloon? It wouldn't take much."

Sadie shook her head. "Where did that come from?"

"You agreed with Marge about trying to keep tourists here. I'm an ideas person. It's what I do for a living. I can help you."

"Why?" Sadie blinked. "Why do that? You're on vacation. A pretty crappy one at that."

Alana gestured dismissively. "I don't have much to do while Noah's working. It would be fun."

"How much longer you gonna be here? It's Wednesday already."

"Oh." Alana did the math and shook her head again. Talk about being delusional. She had only three days left before she returned to New York. Only three days left with Noah. "That's okay," she said, trying to rally her sagging spirits. "I can still do a lot."

Sadie studied her for a moment, then smiled gently. "You're gonna miss him, aren't you?"

"Well, of course I am," Alana said irritably, not anxious to talk about him, or her leaving. "Let's get back to the Watering Hole. Are you interested in the old-time saloon theme? I think it would be a draw for tourists."

"Sounds like a hell of an idea. But, honey, I don't have that kind of money."

"It wouldn't cost much. I bet you have some things in your garage or attic we could use, maybe old wooden signs or even… The ranches around here, they're quite old, aren't they?"

"Been in the same families for over a hundred years, most of them."

"I'm willing to bet they all have attics full of stuff they don't want."

Sadie looked at her thoughtfully. "In the back I have a

sign that belonged to my granddaddy, offering a shave and haircut for two bits."

"Yes, exactly." She turned to measure the room by eye, trying to figure out how much extra space was available. The place was big, the tables and chairs sparse, and she guessed that as time had passed broken furniture hadn't been replaced. On the walls were three posters advertising rodeos and a county fair.

She gestured to an empty corner. "Over here maybe you can have a game of chance—a legal one, of course. We wouldn't want to get the sheriff's boxers in a twist."

"Well, now, how do you know I wear boxers, Ms. Richardson?"

At Noah's gruff question, Alana spun around. He stood just inside the door, not looking as annoyed as he'd sounded. A fond smile tugged at his mouth, and she felt herself flush. "Where did you come from?"

Sadie laughed until she started coughing, but quickly got herself under control. "He knocked and I let him in. You were too busy eyeballing things to notice."

"Am I right about the boxers?" Alana grinned. "It was just a guess, Sheriff."

He shook his head in mock disgust, moving into the room and looking at Sadie. "She giving you any trouble?"

"For pity's sake, the woman has a head full of ideas. Don't know how she intends to pack in so much before she leaves, though."

Alana met Noah's gaze and emotion clogged her throat. In three days she had to say goodbye to this man. How was she going to do that without… She turned away quickly, before she made a complete fool of herself. "I bet you could get Gretchen and Sheila to wear saloon girl costumes, and if you can sew, it shouldn't cost much to keep a selection of dresses to rent to the guests from the Sundance. You can also have theme nights and—"

"Slow down." Sadie chuckled. "Let's see what your man wants."

Alana let out a soft laugh, her mouth open as she darted a look at Noah. He didn't seem offended or uncomfortable or…much of anything, actually. Maybe he was used to Sadie making crazy remarks.

He lifted his hat and readjusted it. "I'll be in the office for a while. Come by later if you want to have lunch. If you're too busy here, no problem."

"Of course she'd rather have lunch with you," Sadie declared. "We're just throwing up some decorations."

Noah hadn't taken his eyes off Alana. "I'm interested in hearing all these ideas she has for the Watering Hole."

"Hey, I have ideas for the whole town," she said, annoyed that she couldn't read him. The man could be so damn straight-faced when it served him.

"It's a shame you won't be here longer," Sadie said. "I bet Marge, Abe and Louise would like to pick your brain. Louise has the sewing shop down the street. She'd want the costume business."

"Sure, I'll meet with her. Abe and Marge, too, if they're interested."

Sadie regarded Noah with a shrewdness that put Alana on alert. "She won't have any time left for you, Sheriff."

His mouth curved in the confident smile of a man who knew better.

"You just might have to talk her into staying for a while longer." Sadie went around the bar and pulled out a stapler from under the register.

"I don't know that I'd be able to swing that," Alana said, keeping her gaze on the older woman. "But it's possible I could come back in a few weeks." She couldn't believe the impulsive thought had slipped out of her mouth. She already had more work than she could handle in New York. Taking off for a long weekend, much less an entire week, was out of the question. And yet...

Noah hadn't said a word, and she wanted to check his reaction, but didn't dare. They hadn't talked about the future. They both understood this was a temporary thing between them, and if he seemed aggravated or panicked, she couldn't stand it. The last thing she wanted was to ruin the few days they had left.

"I know, I know," she said with a flippant laugh. "I'm jumping the gun. I doubt anyone else would be interested. Sometimes I get overly enthusiastic."

"Don't be so sure you wouldn't have takers." This time Noah didn't mask his thoughts, clearly wondering if she was serious about her offer. "People are hurting financially. They've seen the success of the Sundance and they might be willing to listen if you can help them."

"Naturally, I can't guarantee results," she said, trying to ignore the nagging disappointment. It was admirable that he cared about the community, but she'd been hoping for a more personal reaction.

He smiled. "I'm just saying that if you're willing to throw out a line, don't be surprised at the size of your catch."

Alana smiled back. Those sexy eyes of his drove her crazy. Good thing they didn't have a professional relationship. As tough as she was at the office, she doubted she could refuse this man anything.

"Of course, there'll be the naysayers. Or worse, the likes of Avery or Gunderson and the few others who think tourists are the devil's spawn," Sadie said with disgust. "But most folks pay them no mind, anyway."

"Well, ladies, I have to get over to the office," Noah said. But instead of heading for the door, he moved toward Alana.

"I'll be alone. Come whenever." He stopped in front of her, used his forefinger to push back the brim of his hat, then tilted her chin up. And kissed her long and hard.

Holy crap. Right in front of Sadie.

Alana broke away first and silently cleared her throat. "I'll be over in a little while," she murmured.

"Hell, honey, after that kiss, I'd be dragging him into the back room." Sadie's rusty chuckle predictably evolved into a cough, then ended with a mild oath when someone banged on the door.

Noah gestured for her to stay seated. "I'll take care of it, and Alana can lock up behind me. When should I tell them to come back?"

"Another hour. Bet it's Avery." Sadie shook her head. "That man is charging headlong into the drunk tank." Then her face lit with humor. "Let him try arguing with the sheriff."

Noah opened the door to find a wiry older man wearing coveralls a size too big, with his fist in the air, ready to knock again.

He jerked back and frowned accusingly at Noah. "What are you doing here?"

"The bar's not open for another hour, Avery."

The man shot Sadie a reproachful glance. When his gaze moved to Alana, his face crinkled in a pinched expression, cut short by Noah stepping outside and pulling the door closed behind him.

Sadie eyed the oversize wall clock above the shelves of liquor bottles. "Mind locking it?"

Alana had already moved toward the door and made sure the dead bolt was in place. "So that's Avery."

"Yup, but now he won't bother us for the next hour."

"Good. We can get a lot done. I hope you have a ladder."

"Now, look here, honey, I don't wanna take you away from Noah. Gretchen can help me later."

Alana picked up the box. "Come on, Sadie. Do I strike you as a woman who'd let a man think she was too eager?"

Sadie grinned. "No, I reckon you don't." As soon as she turned away, Alana glanced at the clock.

Fifty-eight minutes and counting.

SITTING AT HIS DESK, NOAH stared at the stack of papers in front of him. If he hadn't been so distracted waiting for Alana, he could've knocked off half the reports by now. Man, she'd shocked him. She was thinking about coming back. Twice he'd come close to bringing up the subject, and had chickened out. No use blowing the little time they had left or setting himself up for disappointment.

No doubt her intentions were good, but once she resumed real life, she probably wouldn't give him or Blackfoot Falls a second thought.

That should've suited him just fine. The sex was outstanding, and as much as he'd miss that aspect of their relationship, he plain liked talking to her. He'd confessed more about his feelings toward his mother to Alana than he had to any other human being, and hadn't seen a single trace of judgment in her eyes. She seemed to understand his need to stay emotionally detached, and respected his right to have those feelings.

He supposed he should be more concerned about what the townsfolk thought about him blatantly playing house with her. Ironically, if she had turned out to be a criminal, life would've been easier for him. Eventually he would've arrested her, and everyone would think their sheriff had gone above and beyond to keep their town safe. But this thing between him and Alana had turned personal, and at the end of the day he didn't care what anyone thought. He was on his own time when he was with her, and it was his business. Period.

The office door opened and his heart rate actually increased when he looked up and saw her face. Her cheeks were flushed, her eyes sparkled and she'd pulled her hair back into a messy ponytail. She barely resembled the woman wearing designer clothes and a tense frown who'd come through that door five days ago.

"Too soon?" she asked, her gaze dropping to his cluttered desk. "I can come back."

He threw down his pen. "Get your cute little butt in here and close the blinds."

She grinned and leaned back against the door. "Such a big talker." She pushed off, then glanced out the window before approaching him with a mischievous smile. "Any chance we can go home for lunch?"

Dammit, the way her hips swayed made him think of last night. Of her naked, soft and sweet; of him molding his hand to her curves. "You're gonna be the death of me," he murmured, frustrated that already his jeans had gotten snug.

She slid a hip onto the corner of his desk and leaned toward him for a kiss. He obliged, brushing his lips across hers and then coaxing them apart. Through her T-shirt and bra, he touched her budded nipple.

With a smothered shriek, she jerked back. "Look who's causing trouble now."

"I know." He quickly checked the window to make sure no one had seen them. What the hell was wrong with him? "Hungry?"

"Now how am I supposed to answer that?"

Noah sighed, looked at his watch. "I'm on duty four more hours."

Groaning softly, she ran her gaze over his chest, the raw longing on her face sending more blood surging to his cock. "Don't you have any vacation time?"

Oh, yeah, he knew exactly how much. Last night he'd lain awake while she'd slept, and calculated how he could stretch out the three and a half weeks by grouping the days around holidays. That gave him plenty of leeway to fly to New York a few times.

He caught her hand, and then her gaze. "Is this how you'd want me to use it?"

Alana studied him for a moment, and he could see she was dissecting his words, making sure she understood him. He should've been more plain. What did he have to lose at this point?

"You heard my conversation with Sadie," she said. "What do you think about me coming back?"

"I don't want you to leave."

Her lower lip quivered slightly. "Really?"

As he stood up, she came around the desk and rushed into his arms. He held her against his chest, inhaling the familiar vanilla scent of her hair and sweet warm skin. How quickly he'd gotten used to coming home to her in the evening. Next week was going to be rough.

"I wish I could stay longer," she said, pulling back to look at him. "Maybe I'd be able to squeeze in a couple days, but I have work commitments."

"Of course you do." He smoothed back a stray tendril of hair curling toward her lashes. "I understand you have to leave. Doesn't mean I have to like it."

"I'm completely serious about coming back, and you can visit me in New York."

Before he could answer, the sound of the knob turning alerted them that someone was about to enter the office. They quickly pulled apart, and if the door hadn't stuck slightly, Alana wouldn't have made it to the other side of the desk in time.

Turned out it was only Roy, but Noah still wouldn't have been happy about being caught.

"Afternoon." His deputy whipped off his hat and wiped his

forehead with the back of his sleeve. "Pretty warm out there for the end of October. Can't wait to have me a cold one."

Noah smiled to himself. That was Roy's sly way of hinting he wanted to get off early. Not today. "Was Gus with you?"

"Nope." Roy hung up his hat and smoothed the back of his head even though he didn't have enough hair to worry about. "He's out at the Double R refereeing. A new wrangler had a minor fender bender with Avery Phelps, who's raising Cain over it."

"What was Phelps doing way out there? I saw him trying to get into the Watering Hole less than an hour ago."

"Dunno. But he was acting kinda weird, even for him." Roy opened a folder sitting on top of a stack waiting to be filed. He glanced at Alana and gave her a sheepish smile. "For the record, Ms. Richardson, I never thought it was you."

Alana blinked. "What do you mean?"

Noah's heart crashed to his gut. He hadn't seen any reason to tell her about being a suspect, and now she would wonder why. Casually, he stretched his arms over his head, trying to get Roy's attention.

But it was too late.

16

"THINK IT WAS ME?" ALANA looked from Roy to Noah and back again. "I don't understand."

"That description Sheriff Moran sent us…I'll admit there was a—" Roy's gaze darted to Noah and he stopped talking, his expression abruptly guarded. "Um, guess I shouldn't be shooting my mouth off about office business," he said, his sudden interest in shuffling papers confusing her.

Tempted to push him further, she refrained. No use putting him in a tight spot in front of his boss. But apparently the subject pertained to her, and she'd have to get it out of Noah later.

"I should go see if Gus needs help," Roy muttered, and grabbed his hat. "Avery's in one of those ornery moods."

As soon as the door closed and they were alone, Alana frowned at Noah. She didn't like the grim set of his mouth, and she had a bad feeling he was about to tell her something she'd rather not hear. "What was that about?"

"Why don't you sit down," he said, doing exactly that himself.

She reclaimed her seat, unable to shake the sense of unease.

"Don't look so scared. It's nothing."

"Okay."

"Last Friday, right before you arrived, I received a fax from another sheriff to be on the lookout for a couple of grifters. They'd been working the southern part of the state and fleecing retirees out of their savings." Noah had gone into sheriff mode, his face blank. "Made sense they would head north to Canada. We're less than two hours from the border."

"You said a couple?"

He nodded. "They claimed to be married—whether they were or not didn't matter. Reports said they had split up, that the man had abandoned his partner. And then you showed up without luggage or identification. There was no picture of the woman, just a description that fit you to a T."

Alana stared at him, her mind scrambling to piece the puzzle together. "You thought I was her?"

"I considered the possibility, yes."

"But you verified that I had a reservation at the Sundance under my name."

"For two people who were supposed to have arrived the day before."

"The reservation was Rachel's mistake. As far as arriving late, I explained I missed my flight."

"None of it matters now. Before we went to the McAllisters' I heard she was apprehended." He picked up his tan Stetson and set it on his head. "Let's go get lunch."

Alana's feet couldn't seem to move. Not that she planned on going anywhere. Because it did matter and she had questions that demanded answers. With a flicker of discomfort she flashed back to when she'd first arrived. There had been other women around, guests from the Sundance…yet he'd seemed interested in her. She'd been utterly surprised, but flattered.… She'd flirted, taunted, paraded around in his shirt without a bra. She'd practically thrown herself at him.…

God, she'd been a fool.

She swallowed around the humiliation welling in her throat

and stared directly into his eyes, daring him to look away. "Why did you take me to your house?"

He clearly hated having this conversation. It was there in his darkening expression, but his gaze didn't waver. "To keep an eye on you."

"So..." Her voice cracked a little. "At that point I was a suspect."

"A person of interest would be more accurate." He hesitated, then whipped off his hat, scoring a few points. A cowardly man would've tugged down the brim and obscured his eyes. "Let me show you something."

She watched him leaf through a file, grateful for the few private moments to pull herself together. Maybe she was making too much of this. He was being honest, and they'd come a long way since that first night. Unfortunately, that argument didn't lessen her embarrassment. She felt shame in every pore of her body.

"Here." He held out a sheet of paper. "Take a look."

It was a description that, Alana had to admit, pretty well summed her up. She exhaled a long, shuddering breath. "You received this before I arrived."

He nodded. "Brown hair, brown eyes, tall, thin, attractive, late twenties to early thirties..."

"Hey, early thirties?" She gave him a weak smile.

"Thirties aren't so bad. I haven't picked out a cane yet." Taking the paper from her, he tossed it onto his desk, then pulled her into his arms. "Now, if instead of attractive the description had been drop-dead gorgeous, I would've had no choice but to arrest you."

"Don't push it."

"I haven't lied to you." He tugged on her ponytail. "Although I'll admit, if Roy hadn't opened his big mouth, I might not have mentioned the fax."

The shame hadn't eased much, and when he tried to kiss her she evaded his mouth. "When did you know it wasn't me?"

He loosened his hold, leaning back to give her a long, searching look. "Sunday night. After we had dinner with my folks I was dead sure. Wish I could say it was sooner, but I was doing my job."

Maybe she had no right to feel defensive, especially since he'd been so honest…or had he? How did she know he'd told her everything? "Right."

"You're making too much of this," he said, his good humor gone. "You made things kind of tricky. I tried to get you to call someone for help and you were vague and secretive. Most people in trouble would grab at a lifeline. What was I supposed to think?"

She let out a shaky breath. "No one knew I was coming here. I wanted to keep it that way." She could see that he didn't understand, and she didn't feel compelled to explain further. "I can't imagine what you thought about the way I behaved that first night at your house. Frankly, I'm embarrassed."

Noah let out a sigh as he swiped a hand over his face. "I'm the one who should be embarrassed. You were supposed to be on a nice vacation at a dude ranch, and you weren't here an hour before your whole life was turned upside down. I should have kept my distance, been more professional. But all I could think about was having you in my bed."

Alana felt the pressure in her chest ease. Normally she wouldn't appreciate being objectified, but in Noah's case she'd make an exception.

"Don't look so smug. It was very humbling finding out I'm not the man I thought I was."

"Noah." She didn't know what to say. The longer she studied him, the more serious and distant he seemed to grow. God, she was regretting this conversation, regretted pushing for answers that meant so little in the bigger picture. She'd been embarrassed. So what. "You don't mean that."

His eyes stayed on her, the faintest trace of a challenge in them. Unsettling, because he might as well have reminded her that she didn't know him well enough to pass that judgment.

"I was a damn good cop in Chicago, the youngest uniform ever to be considered for homicide detective. As sheriff I've taken pride in the job I've done here. Until last Friday night… I screwed up."

"No, you didn't. I'm not a criminal." She reached across the desk, hoping he'd take her hand, but it was obvious she'd stirred up something. A big-city cop was one thing, but a homicide detective? Dare she ask why he'd passed up the chance?

"The point is, I didn't know that. Not for sure. But I was still willing to cross the line."

"What about that gut instinct cops are always talking about? That's how you knew I was innocent."

His mouth quirked at the corners. "How many cops do you know?"

She sniffed. "I watch TV occasionally."

Finally, a true smile reached his eyes. "Look, I didn't mean to take that detour." He stood again. "I promised you lunch."

"Do you ever miss Chicago?"

"Not so much. I miss the job, but I'm not partial to city living." He came around the desk and pulled her to her feet. "Marge's or home for lunch?"

She'd hoped for another answer. But she was thankful the mood had lightened. Still, it bothered her that he doubted himself in any way, and she resolved that they would talk more later. "Hmm, let's see, Marge's or the privacy of your bedroom—oops, I meant kitchen."

Conflicting emotions washed across his face, then Noah

wrapped his arms around her and hugged her. "You're an amazing woman, Alana. I admire the hell out of you."

His words took her aback. If she'd expected him to say anything it wasn't that. "Amazing? Not always," she said with a laugh, "believe me." She leaned back to look at him, something he must not have wanted her to do, because his arms tightened. "I don't think I've met a more confident man in my life."

He pulled her closer and kissed her hair. "I want you to come back," he whispered. "I'll always want you to come back. But I understand this isn't your world. That it could never be."

She tried to come up with an argument, and hated that she couldn't find one.

THEY NEVER DID MAKE IT TO HIS place. It was absurd how a town as small as Blackfoot Falls had so many people who demanded their sheriff's attention. Noah claimed it wasn't always like this. Just Alana's luck that everyone had chosen this week to ruin her plans.

Okay, so maybe she was taking it a little too personally, but all of a sudden it felt as if her vacation would be over in ten minutes, and she wanted to spend every second with him. Until today they'd carefully avoided any talk of the future. Rightfully so, but now she had so many questions it was hard to concentrate on the simple task of hanging paper witches from the large elm in the center of town.

After she'd finished putting up the rest of Sadie's decorations, Alana volunteered her services to the Lemon sisters. The elderly twins could agree on absolutely nothing. It was a wonder they'd decorated most of Main Street by themselves.

When the wind had taken down the ghosts, the sisters had decided to replace them with the witches. Alana couldn't see letting either Mabel or Miriam navigate the ladder. Although she had a feeling neither one had had any intention of doing the climbing.

"Make sure that one is tied good and tight." Mabel, the more anal of the two, pointed to a witch dangling from the highest branch reachable from the ancient ladder, which she was in charge of holding.

"It's fine," Alana said. "I don't need to check it."

Mabel squinted, the disapproval clear in her lined face, her free hand going to her plump hip.

Sighing, Alana tugged up the loose waist of her jeans.

"I'm sorry, dear, but I think Mabel is right," Miriam said sweetly, peering up from under the shade of the bright pink umbrella she held.

Now they finally agreed on something. Terrific.

Alana started to argue, but decided it would be easier to do as they asked. Then she'd climb down, and that was it for her. Noah would be off duty in an hour and she wanted to clean up. Her hair was a mess and her T-shirt was clinging to her sweaty back.

She'd made it to the last rung of the ladder when both women turned their heads toward the south of town. Alana followed their curious gazes and saw a big, shiny silver car gliding slowly down Main. Despite the sisters' interest, all she cared about was seeing Noah.

She jumped off the ladder, grateful for the track shoes Rachel had given her on Monday night. Alana didn't care so much that she'd been on the verge of totally wrecking her expensive heels, just that the sneakers were comfortable. Yet another thing that made her realize how different she'd become once she'd landed in Blackfoot Falls.

"I'll put away the ladder," she said, taking it from a preoccupied Mabel. "You'll have to tell me where."

The older woman seemed far more concerned with the

Cadillac. "Who *is* that?" she asked, without so much as a glance at Miriam or Alana. "She can't be from around here."

Both sisters seemed so startled that Alana gave in and turned around.

The ladder nearly slipped from her hands. She tightened her hold, clinging as if her life depended on it.

Dressed in a chic black suit, Eleanor stood beside the parked Cadillac, her hand on the open driver's door. She closed it as she panned the storefronts, her gaze briefly touching on Alana, then moving on to a group of cowboys standing outside the Watering Hole. With a sudden start, Eleanor did a double take and looked back at Alana.

Vaguely aware that she'd rudely shoved the ladder at Mabel, Alana pulled her hair free of the ponytail, shook it out and smoothed her untucked T-shirt. What the hell was her mother doing here? How had she known where to come...?

Eleanor was too far away for Alana to see her eyes clearly, but that didn't matter. Her mother had to be as stunned as she was. No, Alana won the shock award. At least Eleanor had apparently expected to see her.

"You know her?" Mabel asked. Alana ignored the woman.

Everyone was looking now. The guys outside Sadie's, kids from the high school.

Of course they would. Eleanor made quite a picture with her perfect blond hair pinned up into a perfect French twist. Her suit had been custom tailored in Hong Kong and her designer heels probably cost more than the battered blue pickup parked behind her.

This was crazy. If everyone hadn't been staring, Alana might've convinced herself this was a hallucination. With her stomach tied in knots, she forced her feet to move. Her mother hadn't budged an inch. Alana hadn't expected her to. After all, she wasn't the one who'd disappointed.

Hating that they had an audience, Alana made sure she

got close enough to keep their conversation private. "What are you doing here, Eleanor?"

"Me?" Her mother ran her gaze over Alana. Distaste flickered in her face. Normally it wasn't easy getting a reaction out of her. "I was worried sick about you. Do you know how many times I called and left voice mails?"

"I sent you a message before I left New York."

"Yes, you did." A perfectly arched brow lifted. "And you lied about where you were going." Her shoulders drew back and she swept a quick glance toward the Watering Hole. "It's not necessary to have this conversation out here. Where is your hotel?"

Alana drew in a shaky breath, sneaking a peek around. The Lemon sisters had moved closer, dragging the ladder with them. God. Where the hell was she going to take Eleanor for privacy? Though the truth was, she had nothing to say. Alana didn't owe her an explanation. It was the other way around. All Alana wanted to do was scream at the top of her lungs for her mother to go away.

Eleanor stared at the shirt and Levi's. "Why are you wearing those things?" she asked in a low, irate voice, as if she couldn't help herself. As if she no longer had control over her carefully modulated tone.

"My luggage was stolen."

Her mother's lips parted slightly and something registered in her hazel eyes, as though she'd just made a connection. "Get in the car. I'll take you to your hotel."

"I'm sorry you drove all the way out here for nothing," Alana said in an admirably calm voice. The last thing she wanted was to become a spectacle on Main Street again, but she had nowhere to go. Certainly not to Noah's house. The panic-inducing thought raced along the edges of her nerves. "There is no hotel in Blackfoot Falls. If you turn around now you may find one before dark."

Eleanor's gaze narrowed in disbelief. "What's happened to you?"

"Nothing. I'm fine."

"No, you aren't." Her mother's unfailing composure momentarily slipped. "Let me help you," she said urgently, her gaze flicking to something over Alana's shoulder. "Just please get in the car. Tell me where you're staying, and we'll go from there."

Controlling the impulse to turn and run as far as she could, Alana drew in a deep breath. There was no way this would end well, no matter what she said. But she could mitigate the fallout. "I'm staying at a dude ranch."

"A what?"

"I'm sure you know what a dude ranch is."

Eleanor just stared at her, no noticeable disapproval on her face, at least not to someone who didn't know her well. What did unnerve Alana was the banked hostility she'd never before seen in her mother's eyes. "Fine. How far is it?"

Alana had to think fast. She could call Rachel...explain enough to get a room for each of them. Just for tonight...

Another thought stopped her cold, such an unpleasant one that it made her stomach cramp. "How did you find me?"

"I told you this conversation can wait."

"You had my cell phone tracked," Alana said, the pain in her belly growing nearly unbearable. Her mother had finally crossed the line. "Didn't you?"

"What? That's ridiculous." She waved a hand impatiently and opened the car door. "How would I do such a thing?"

Alana didn't move. "Oh, please."

Eleanor shook her head and stared at her as if she'd never seen her before. And then, for a brief moment, concern settled into her features. "Some crazy old man answered the last time I called. He told me he lived in Blackfoot Falls, Montana. Now for the love of God, would you get in the—" Abruptly, she jerked her head and glared at something behind Alana. "This is a private conversation."

Alana spun around.

Noah stood not three feet away. Looking at Eleanor, he touched the brim of his hat. "Afternoon, ma'am," he said, cool as could be, then shifted his gaze. "Alana, everything all right?"

She opened her mouth, but hesitated long enough for her mother to jump in.

"You're the sheriff, I presume. What have you done about my daughter's missing luggage?"

"Eleanor, stop." Alana paused, forced herself to breathe. "Sheriff Calder has been very helpful. He even made sure I had a room at the Sundance Dude Ranch." She cleared her throat and slid him a glance. He was watching her with detached interest. Jesus, he and her mother, what a pair. God forbid they should show their emotions.

Except she knew what Noah was feeling right now. Hurt and confused. She'd referred to him as Sheriff Calder, as if he were no more than a civil servant to her. And then lied about where she'd been staying, as if she was ashamed to admit the truth. He had to understand her predicament, though, now that he knew this was her mother.

Noah took out the pen and small notebook he kept in his breast pocket. "I overheard you say a man answered Ms. Richardson's phone," he said in a deceptively businesslike manner. "Anything you remember about his voice or what he said that might help identify him?"

Alana heard her mother answer, but she didn't pay attention to the words. All she could do was stare at Noah, with icy fingers of dread squeezing her heart. He didn't get it. He was angry and hurt, and she couldn't do a damn thing about it until she got rid of Eleanor.

17

NOAH SAID NOTHING AS HE AND Alana walked toward his office. Her mother was sitting in the Caddy, no doubt watching them like a hawk. If he hadn't seen with his own eyes how Alana behaved around her he wouldn't have believed it. Any parent-child relationship could be complicated, but Alana's inability to hold her own in the face of Eleanor had surprised the hell out of him. Especially after he'd seen her in action with Gunderson. The strong, capable woman he'd begun to know had reminded him of a rebellious teenager struggling to cut the cord. She didn't want to give in, but she wasn't ready to draw a line in the sand, either.

"You're angry, and I'm sorry. I don't blame you," she said the second they entered his office and closed the door.

"I'm not angry." He took off his hat. "You want me to call Rachel, or do you want to do it?"

Alana folded her arms across her chest. "I couldn't tell her I was staying with you, because then…" Her shoulders sagged and she cast a helpless look out the window. "Believe me, this is the path of least resistance. I'll spend the night with her at the Sundance. She'll leave first thing tomorrow, and I'll come back to town."

"You don't owe me an explanation." When he almost added

that he was *only* the local sheriff, he realized he was a little angry…and hurt. Shit. They just had a few days left…. "Here's the number to the Sundance."

"Noah." She tugged at his arm. "Please."

"What?"

"Kiss me?"

He glanced toward the window, wondering if Eleanor had stayed put as her daughter had asked. When he looked into Alana's pleading eyes, the misery he saw there softened him, and he finger-combed the tangles away from her flushed cheeks.

"I'll make this up to you, I swear." She rose on tiptoe, and he met her partway, brushing his lips across hers. "I'll call Rachel myself. Did you figure out who took my luggage?"

"I have a hunch."

She didn't ask who he thought it was, which was just as well, because he wasn't about to throw a name around without proof. There was still some shred of lawman in him.

He left her in the office using the phone, and considered the idea that this could be the last time he ever saw her. She had nothing at his house of any value, and if her mother pushed hard enough, he wouldn't be surprised if Alana took off for New York with her tomorrow morning.

Just as quickly he discarded the notion. Not the leaving tomorrow, that was a solid possibility. But she wouldn't simply disappear without saying goodbye to him. Oh, he had no illusions that she would admit the truth about their brief fling. No reason to, really, but if keeping the secret meant she'd have to leave early, he didn't see her coming clean in order to justify staying.

Noah let out a heavy sigh. Hell, he understood keeping secrets. Nobody in town talked about his mother's drinking, at least not to his face. She rarely left the ranch anymore, and somehow he and his sisters had convinced themselves that no one knew about Celia Calder's decline. They'd kept her out of sight, under the guise of keeping her safe.

Yeah, Alana thought he was a great son. Right. Easy to be Zen when you can shove the problem under the rug. Keep it nice and tidy and compartmentalized, separate from your daily life. Nah, that wasn't true. He was doing right by his mother.

Before he climbed into his truck, he stopped at the Watering Hole. No one had seen Avery since Noah had barred him from bothering Sadie earlier. Good. He'd rather confront the old man at his ranch and not before an audience. Not because Noah thought he might be wrong about the man. Made sense it was someone like Avery. The old man was angry and lonely and aching to hit someone who couldn't hit back. He'd probably seen a chance and gone for it.

Noah turned off onto Avery's gravel road, which was sorely in need of grading. The truck bounced over deep potholes that were going to be hell to cross come winter, after the first major snow. If Avery used a quarter of the time he spent drinking to maintain the place, maybe he wouldn't be so miserable.

The run-down cabin-style home came into view, the small spread looking deserted until Noah spotted his quarry's truck parked on the side of the house closest to the barn. He pulled alongside the rusty clunker, got out and looked around. The place really needed work, although it wasn't used for much anymore other than to keep a roof over Avery's head and house his chickens and last cow.

Before Noah had to knock, Avery opened the front door, rubbing his eyes as if he'd been sleeping. He shuffled in his stockinged feet onto the porch. Usually he wore coveralls instead of dungarees. One of his suspenders had slid off his narrow shoulder and he snapped it back into place.

"What are you doing here?" he asked in the cantankerous

tone that made people want to wring his neck. He stopped at the edge of the porch, spit into the dirt. "You bring that filly with you?" He craned his neck toward Noah's truck. "Or did she give you the boot already?" He smiled slyly. "You shoulda known better, Calder. That one's a Thoroughbred."

Noah gritted his teeth. No way would he let the man rattle him. "I need you to do something for me."

His weathered face creased into a suspicious frown.

"I want you to let me inside."

Avery stumbled back a step. "This is private property."

"You have a problem showing me what you got in there?"

"Damn right I do."

"You wouldn't have something that doesn't belong to you, would you?" Noah asked calmly, and saw fear creep into Avery's small dark eyes. "Like some luggage and a purse?"

"I ain't got anything you need worry about." He moved to block the door.

"There's a lady in town who says different. Seems she had a real nice phone conversation with you."

Avery's face lit up. "She's here? Is she pretty?"

Noah heaved a tired sigh. Maybe someday he'd laugh about this. "Move aside, Phelps."

He blinked rapidly and shook his head. "You got no call to make me let you in my house."

"I'm asking nicely, because one way or another, I'm gonna have a look, you understand?"

"Don't you need one of those warrants?" Avery must've recognized Noah's exasperation because he lifted his gray-whiskered chin with renewed confidence. "I reckon I'd like to see one of those pieces of paper, Sheriff."

Noah took off his hat, stared at it while he fingered the brim, and tried to regain control of his rising temper. He had to remain professional, forget the remark about Alana being a Thoroughbred.

After taking a deep breath, he looked up at Avery's smug face. "Force me to get a warrant, and I'll cuff you to the goddam bumper of my truck and make you walk to town."

RACHEL'S DIRECTIONS TO THE Sundance were perfect, and if Eleanor harbored any suspicion that Alana hadn't been staying there all along, she kept it to herself on the largely silent drive out to the ranch. Good thing, because Alana's mind was racing crazily. Rachel had no spare rooms, but she'd kindly offered to make up one in the family quarters.

At first Alana was horrified that she would have no choice but to share the room with Eleanor. But cool, calm, wonderful Rachel had offered her the couch in the den. It was for only one night, and it worked out beautifully, because if they did share, it would be obvious to Eleanor that Alana had not been staying there. But instead, when they parted company at the end of the evening, Eleanor would assume Alana was going to her own room.

The sun had dipped low by the time they arrived. Floodlights were already turned on outside the house and both barns. The front of the three-story house consisted of an amazing expanse of windows—odd for a place that got so cold in winter, but it made for stunning views of the Rockies in the distance.

As Eleanor parked the car alongside a row of other rentals, Rachel stepped onto the large wraparound porch. The sight of her welcoming smile brought a lump to Alana's throat. She barely knew Noah's friend, and yet the woman had bent over backward to help.

"Hi," Alana said, climbing out of the car and trying hard to hide her nerves. *"Thank you,"* she mouthed to Rachel over the roof of the Cadillac as her mother gathered her purse and opened the driver's door.

Eleanor took an inordinate amount of time stepping out

of the car and around the patches of dirt. Alana wanted to make the introductions, but waited with a clenched jaw for her mother to find an acceptable grassy spot on which to stand.

"I'm sure Alana has explained that we don't have any vacant rooms in the guest wing," Rachel said smoothly. "I had to put you on the same floor with the family, but I think you'll be comfortable."

Eleanor cast a critical eye toward the house, then offered the benign smile she generally saved for doormen and waitstaff. "I'm sure it will be fine."

"Well." Rachel rubbed a palm down the front of her jeans. "We're about to serve dinner. You two hungry?"

"I'd prefer to go to my room," Eleanor said quickly. "I'll have something light later."

Meeting Rachel's startled gaze, Alana felt the heat crawling up her neck. "This isn't the Ritz, Eleanor. You eat when they serve."

"Don't worry about it," Rachel said, pretending she hadn't seen Eleanor's expression tighten. "We'll have something for you later. Let's go get you settled."

"You have someone to bring my bag?"

Alana had seen the small Louis Vuitton overnight bag in the backseat. For God's sake. "I'll get it," she said.

At the same time Rachel said, "Yes, someone will bring it right up."

Eleanor seemed momentarily confused. Was someone who was so intelligent really that clueless? It was weird seeing her out of her element.

Their element. The thought unsettled Alana. But the fact was, *her* life was full of similar expectations. Up until five days ago, when she'd slipped down the rabbit hole.

Rachel was frowning at something. "I think that's Noah."

Just hearing his name was enough to start Alana's heart

fluttering, and she shifted her gaze in time to see a truck turn off the road onto the long gravel driveway.

"Do we need to wait out here?" Eleanor asked. "Surely he's not come to see us."

"Go on inside," Alana said, not keen on being around him in front of her mother in any case. "After what you told him, he may have information about my luggage."

"Right." Eleanor studied her a bit too closely. "I'll wait with you."

Alana knew it was no use arguing. She'd already ignited her mother's curiosity. Aware that Rachel was watching them, she felt shame wash over her, and averted her gaze. Her mother had behaved like an ass, and Alana, well, here she was a grown woman still cowed by her. Temporarily, of course, to avoid a scene. Everyone would understand later.

The three of them waited in silence while Noah drove up, then stopped a few feet away. Through his tinted windows, Alana could tell someone else was sitting in the cab, but she couldn't see who.

Noah stepped out of the truck. He got something from the backseat, and when he cleared the pickup, she saw her luggage and purse.

Letting out a small shriek, she raced toward him. "You found it! I can't believe... I'd given up hope." She threw her arms around Noah, then remembered she had an audience and quickly backed off. "Is everything there?"

"You'll have to tell me," he said, passing over her purse and studying her face. His eyes were difficult to see under the brim of his hat, especially because, unlike her, he was standing in the shadow of the house.

She lowered her lashes and concentrated on inventorying her things. "You can put the bag down. It has wheels."

"Why don't I take it to the porch so it doesn't get dirty?"

Alana slung her purse over her shoulder and reached for

her laptop case. "I think we're too late for that." She felt her mother's gaze burning a hole in her back. "I'll just take it inside now."

"Who's that in the truck?" Rachel asked.

Noah turned briefly to throw a disgusted look toward his passenger. "Avery. I have to take him to my office. Start writing up the paperwork to charge him."

"Isn't this evidence?" Alana asked, nodding at her luggage and purse.

"Yeah, technically." Noah gave a small guilty shrug and glanced at Eleanor. "I figured you need your things, so don't worry about it. I'll make it work."

The sound of the truck door opening drew everyone's attention. Avery ambled around the hood, his bowlegged gait slowing him down. His eyes went to Eleanor and lit up. He spit into his palm and smoothed back his wiry hair. Alana heard her mother's soft gasp of disgust.

"Dammit, Avery, what did I tell you?" Noah said, his voice low and stern. "Get back in the truck or I'm cuffing you."

"I just wanna apologize to Miss Alana, Sheriff." He looked over, but had trouble meeting her eyes. "Didn't mean no harm." Then he grinned at Eleanor. "You're even prettier than you sounded on the phone."

That startled a laugh out of Alana.

Her mother stiffened. "I'd like to go inside now," she said in a voice that brooked no argument. Ignoring Avery, Noah and even Rachel, she gave Alana a censuring gaze. "Coming?"

Alana gripped her purse strap tighter. "I'll take this," she said, not surprised when Noah promptly released the handle of her bag. "Thank you," she added, hoping desperately that by the time she had a chance to explain, he'd still want to hear it. She met his eyes, then wished she hadn't. Hard to miss his disappointment. "I'll see you tomorrow."

Her heart sank when he looked as if he didn't believe her.

"I CAN'T IMAGINE HOW YOU withstood being stuck here for this long." Eleanor shook out her silky nightgown and carefully laid it on the bed, which was covered by a quaint patchwork quilt she'd already made a condescending remark about. Thankfully, not in front of Rachel. "You should've called me immediately."

Alana merely picked up her mother's designer toiletry bag and carried it to the attached bathroom, which hadn't met with her approval, either.

"Why didn't you call me when everything got stolen? That sheriff..." Her mother waved a dismissive hand. "Whatever his name was, didn't he offer you a phone call? He certainly seemed accommodating enough."

Oh, Alana wasn't fooled by Eleanor's show of indifference. She'd sensed the spark between Alana and Noah, and now Eleanor was fishing. Alana felt too numb to care. All she could think about was how horribly she'd disappointed him. How profoundly disappointed she was in herself.

Funny how in Blackfoot Falls, Eleanor's cracks showed so glaringly. In her own world, she was a star. She needed only to smile and accept the praise. In the real world, she was awful—intolerant, judgmental, completely out of touch with how most people lived.

"When are you going to change out of those horrid clothes?" Eleanor called out, and Alana realized she was still standing in the bathroom, finding it hard to meet her own gaze in the mirror. "I understand why you would want to have everything washed or dry-cleaned first, but surely there's something in your suitcase that would do for now."

Alana finally raised her eyes to her reflection, and what she saw shamed her. She'd gotten it all wrong. Eleanor hadn't embarrassed her; Alana had embarrassed herself. She could try to blame her unspeakably childish behavior on her mother's unexpected arrival, but that was crap.

She was just as guilty as the rest of Eleanor's sycophants, treating her mother as if she were above the use of courtesy or compassion. When had she ever stood up to the woman? Alana had spent her life ignoring her, evading her, taking petty vengeance with passive-aggressive behavior. But had she ever made a stand and fought for something she wanted? How had she put it to Rachel? Better to take the path of least resistance?

God, even her assistant had seen through her. Pam knew Alana was incapable of saying no to Eleanor. Why was it so easy to stand up to strangers, when the only relationship that was truly hurting her was the one with her mother?

And now Alana had hurt Noah. He'd taken her home to dinner without a whisper about his mom's problem. He hadn't been embarrassed by her. He lived his life, and he left his mom to live hers.

Eleanor was still going on about something, but Alana had quit listening. Time to fight for what she wanted, and the hell with letting her mother stand in her way.

"Hey, Mom," she said as she left the bathroom. "You do know your way back to the airport, yes?"

Eleanor gaped at her. "What? Is something wrong?"

"I hope not." Alana smiled and kissed her cheek. "I'll see you in New York."

"Excuse me?" Her expression grew furious.

"Have a safe trip," Alana said, and slipped out the door. She had to find Rachel, her luggage and a ride to town.

IRRITABLE AND DEPRESSED, NOAH slammed the door between his office and the cell where Avery had been bellyaching for the past two hours. The man hadn't shut up since they left the Sundance. Not only that, but Noah knew he was in for a chewing out from the judge. He'd had no business releasing evidence, but he'd wanted to see Alana, mostly for reassur-

ance. A lot of good that had done. Now he was more certain
than ever that she'd be out of here tomorrow. If she stopped
in Blackfoot Falls at all it would be only to sign a statement
against Avery. She'd say goodbye, talk about a return trip,
but he couldn't see it.

He'd like to convince her otherwise, but then what did he
have to offer her? He wasn't willing to move to New York,
and her life was there, not here, or anyplace resembling Blackfoot Falls. Besides, they barely knew each other. What had
it been, five days?

He sat at his desk and rubbed his throbbing temples. This
afternoon he'd been convinced that he knew her well. They'd
shared so much, so easily. But she'd acted so strangely with
her mother. The difference between the woman putting
Gunderson in his place and the girl twisting herself in knots
for her mother was like night and day. If he hadn't witnessed
it himself, he'd never have believed it.

Damn.

He still felt as if he knew her, but he didn't comprehend
the dynamic of that relationship, not one bit. He'd seen her
with Sadie and his mother, though, and knew that Alana had
a good heart. She was smart and quick, and he understood
her in ways he couldn't explain, but he knew there was more
to learn. Maybe someday… If they had more time together…

Man, going home tonight was gonna be a bitch. Not just
because the house would be empty, but Alana wouldn't be
there to ask about his day, tell him about her plans for the
Watering Hole. She wouldn't be there, eyes sparkling, standing on tiptoes waiting for his kiss.

Forcing in a deep breath, he stared at the paperwork sum-
marizing the charges against Avery. Noah hadn't finished yet,
but it was no use; staring wasn't improving his concentration.
He had to do something. Like drive out to the Sundance and

talk to Alana in private. He threw down his pen and pushed back from his desk.

Damned if he knew what he was going to say....

He heard the door open, stick for a second, and then he saw Alana. She looked different dressed in tailored black slacks and a red turtleneck sweater, her designer purse slung over her shoulder.

"I was hoping I'd catch you here," she said, smiling nervously and closing the door behind her.

"I didn't expect to see you tonight."

"No, I don't suppose you would have." She moved to the guest chair and sat down, and he flashed back on last Friday. Probably because she looked more like that woman who'd first sat across from him—mysterious, disheveled, and still so captivating he'd marched right past his own rules in order to be close to her.

He could barely believe how hard his heart was pounding now that she was back in that chair. He wanted so badly for this not to be goodbye.

Her gaze lowered to the report. "I don't want to press charges against Avery."

"He stole from you, no matter what his reasons were." Confused, Noah watched her fidget with the strap of her purse. "No one will blame you for lodging a complaint. Legally, he has to answer for his actions."

"Look, as far as I'm concerned, it was a misunderstanding. I won't sign a statement against him."

"A misunderstanding?" Was this about not wanting to return for the trial? The thought depressed Noah all over again. "You won't have to come back to testify, if that's what you're worried about. Avery admitted everything, said he was trying to hurt the Sundance and keep tourists away."

"You know," she said, leaning forward, "I have every intention of returning. And when I do I'd like to find the town and everyone in it just as they were before." She smiled. "I'm with Avery. I don't want to see tourists like Eleanor ruining things." Alana moistened her lips. "Tourists like me." Her chin lifted and her eyes blazed as she smiled. "But that's just too bad, because I'm coming back, anyway."

Noah felt his own smile spread across his face. "Did your mother come with you?"

"No," Alana said, her back ramrod straight. "I told her to go back where she belongs first thing tomorrow. Rachel dropped me off."

"Ah." Noah got to his feet. "So where are you staying tonight?"

"Well, I heard there's this hot sheriff who takes in strays," she said, rising from the chair.

"Is that right?" He caught her hand and pulled her toward him, the tension melting at the feel of her lush warm body pressed to his.

She slid her arms around his neck and smiled up at him. "Besides, you have my clothes."

"You have your luggage."

"Oh, please, I have nothing appropriate for the fall festival on Friday." She stretched up and kissed him, firmly but briefly. "I have no idea where this thing between us is going…." She hesitated. "Your input about now would be welcome."

Noah stroked her back. "I don't know, either, but I'm willing to keep doing what we've been doing until we figure it out."

"It's going to require some traveling back and forth for both of us."

He smiled. "Is that a problem for you?"

She shook her head. "The problem would be never seeing you again."

Lowering his head, he whispered, "You're the best thing that's ever happened to Blackfoot Falls."

Her head tilted slightly. "So you want me back just to help out the town?"

"Hang the town. I want you back for me."

The way her lips parted on a gasp made it impossible not to kiss her. And kiss her.

And kiss her....

* * * * *

Return to Blackfoot Falls in December with
ON A SNOWY CHRISTMAS NIGHT, the third book in
Debbi Rawlins's MADE IN MONTANA *miniseries. You're*
sure to fall in love with dark, sexy cowboy
Jesse McAllister!

REQUEST YOUR FREE BOOKS!
2 FREE NOVELS PLUS 2 FREE GIFTS!

red-hot reads!

*Bestselling Harlequin® Blaze™ author Rhonda Nelson
is back with yet another irresistible Man out of Uniform.
Meet Jebb Willington—former ranger, current security
agent and all-around good guy. His assignment—to catch
a thief at an upscale retirement residence. The problem—
he's falling for sexy massage therapist Sophie O'Brien,
the woman he's trying to put behind bars....*

*Read on for a sneak peek at
THE PROFESSIONAL*

Available November 2012 only from Harlequin Blaze.

Oh, hell.

Former ranger Jeb Willingham didn't need extensive army training to recognize the telltale sound that emerged roughly ten feet behind him. He was Southern, after all, and any born-and-bred Georgia boy worth his salt would recognize the distinct metallic click of a 12-gauge shotgun. And given the decided assuredness of the action, he knew whoever had him in their sights was familiar with the gun and, more important, knew how to use it.

"On your feet, hands where I can see them," she ordered. He had to hand it to her. Sophie O'Brien was cool as a cucumber. Her voice was steady, not betraying the slightest bit of fear. Which, irrationally, irritated him. He was a strange man trespassing on her property—she ought to be afraid, dammit. Why hadn't she stayed in the house and called 911 like a normal woman?

Oh, right, he thought sarcastically. Because she wasn't a *normal* woman. She was kind and confident, fiendishly clever and sexy as hell.

He wanted her.

And the hell of it? Aside from the conflict of interest and the tiny matter of *her name at the top of his suspect list?*

She didn't like him.

"Move," she said again, her voice firmer. "I'd rather not shoot you, but I will if you don't stand up and turn around."

Beautiful, Jeb thought, feeling extraordinarily stupid. He'd been an army ranger, one of the fiercest soldiers among Uncle Sam's finest...and he'd been bested by a massage therapist with an Annie Oakley complex.

With a sigh, he got up and flashed a grin at her. "Evening, Sophie. Your shrubs need mulching."

She gasped, betraying the first bit of surprise. It was ridiculous how much that pleased him. "You?" she breathed. "What the hell are you doing out here?"

He pasted a reassuring look on his face and gestured to the gun still aimed at his chest. "Would you mind lowering your weapon? It's a bit unnerving."

She brought the barrel down until it was aimed directly at his groin. "There," she said, a smirk in her voice. "Feel better?"

Has Jebb finally met his match? Find out in
THE PROFESSIONAL

Available November 2012
wherever Harlequin Blaze books are sold.

Find yourself
BANISHED TO THE HAREM
in a glamorous and tantalizing new tale from

Carol Marinelli

Playboy Sheikh Prince Rakhal Alzirz has time for
one more fling in London before he must return
to his desert kingdom—and Natasha Winters has
caught his eye. He seizes the chance to discover if
Natasha is as fiery in bed as her flaming red hair,
but their recklessness has consequences.... She
might be carrying the Alzirz heir!

BANISHED
TO THE HAREM

Available October 16!